Amen, L.A.

Amen, L.A.

Cherie Bennett *and* Jeff Gottesfeld

Ember

Text copyright © 2011 by Cherie Bennett

All rights reserved. Published in the United States by Ember, an imprint of Random House Children's Books, a division of Random House, Inc., New York.

Ember and the colophon are trademarks of Random House, Inc.

www.randomhouse.com/teens

Educators and librarians, for a variety of teaching tools, visit us at
www.randomhouse.com/teachers

Library of Congress Cataloging-in-Publication Data
Bennett, Cherie.
Amen, L.A. / by Cherie Bennett & Jeff Gottesfeld — 1st Ember ed.
p. cm.
Summary: When seventeen-year-old Natalie Shelton and her familiy move from Minnesota to Beverly Hills after her mother is hired as pastor of the wealthy Church of Beverly Hills, Natalie becomes overwhelmed by the lavish lifestyle and starts to forget her Christian values.
ISBN 978-0-385-73188-1 (trade pbk.) — ISBN 978-0-385-90225-0 (lib. bdg.) —
ISBN 978-0-375-89808-2 (ebook)
[1. Conduct of life—Fiction. 2. Christian life—Fiction. 3. Beverly Hills (Calif.)—Fiction.]
I. Gottesfeld, Jeff. II. Title.
PZ7.B43912Am 2011
[Fic]—dc22
2010032348

RL: 6.0

Printed in the United States of America

10 9 8 7 6 5 4 3 2 1

First Ember Edition 2011

Random House Children's Books supports the First Amendment
and celebrates the right to read.

For our editor,
Wendy Loggia. Amen!

Prologue

To lose my virginity or not to lose my virginity? That was the question.

Before I elaborate, I really should introduce myself—my name is Natalie Shelton, but my friends call me Nat—and let you get to know this virgin on the verge. Now, I don't normally blab about my personal life to complete strangers. In fact, one of my pet peeves is when a girl you've never seen before decides that just because you happen to end up in the same ladies' room at the same time, this is the moral equivalent of longtime best-friend-hood, and she spills the most intimate details of her life. Her period is late and she's scared to death she's pregnant. Or she has certain—ahem—symptoms that make her worry she has an STD but no way can she go to the family doctor because the family doctor is her mom's best friend. Or . . . well, you get the idea.

No matter how many times this happens—and it happens

to me *a lot*—I'm still amazed. My dad says I just have a face, like my mother's, that makes people feel like they can confide in me. My mom and I both have deep-set blue eyes, a round face with dimples inherited from my grandma Palma, and shoulder-length wavy blondish hair. I say "blondish" because in my case, it's the color you end up with when you're a platinum-blond baby and everyone coos over you and says how cute you are and how gorgeous your hair is and how you look like a little angel that should be on the top of a Christmas tree, only then you grow up and by the time you're seventeen and filling out the information for the driver's license your parents have *finally* allowed you to get, when you write *blond* under hair color, you're kinda-sorta-almost-but-not-quite lying.

In my mom's case, it's Clairol Nice 'n Easy.

I guess that's what I have to look forward to. Joy.

Once I got past the baby-pudge stage—which lasted until I was fourteen, unlike for my younger brother and sister, who each apparently reached puberty in the womb—and shot up to my present height of five foot six, I ended up with a decent figure and nice legs. Once, at a party, this guy told me I look like Katherine Heigl. He also told me he wasn't wearing his contact lenses. Objectively, I suppose I'm not as hot as my little—trust me, "little" refers only to the fact that she's two years younger than me—sister, Gemma. She's five eight but has four-inch heels, like, superglued to her feet, and one of those skinny-curvy-busty-all-natural bodies that get a million guys wanting to be your friend on Facebook. Her goal in life is to be famous. She worships Megan Fox. Unfortunately, I'm totally serious.

As for my brother, Chad, he's also little in name only. Already five foot nine (thanks to Grandpa Chester) at age thirteen and still growing, with black hair and huge blue eyes framed by long, sooty lashes, he's got a cut, broad-shouldered swimmer's build, because, well, he's a swimmer. One of the best his age in the state of Minnesota. Mostly, he concentrates on swimming, which is a good thing. If he concentrated on girls, Mankato would be the broken-heart capital of the Midwest. Again, totally serious.

My dad, Charlie, is an author of middlingly successful mysteries. No bestsellers, but he does write for a New York publishing house and has a rabid, if modest, following. My mom, Marsha, who I sort of look like, is a minister. The "my mom is a minister" thing had everything to do with why I was pondering the big "Do I or don't I?"

Hang on, this is all going to make sense, I swear.

At the moment of my contemplation, I was on the bedroom floor of my good friend Shelby's family fishing cabin on the shore of Lake Washington, about forty-five minutes from Mankato. I was separated from the hardwood floor by a truly butt-ugly pee-yellow/puke-green hooked rug and could hear my friends partying in the living room while Lady Gaga sang. My red blouse was off, my floral summer skirt had worked its way up to my navel, and my boyfriend Sean's hands were inching under my 36B lacy pink push-up bra bought on sale at Victoria's Secret—the one my mother didn't know I owned.

My position—on the floor—and the position of Sean's hands—on my breasts—would have been shocking to those on the other side of the bedroom door. Here's the thing. I am the proverbial "good girl." Good grades, good friends, a good relationship with my mom and dad, do church volunteer work, play guitar and write songs, don't drink, don't smoke anything, don't do drugs, and the gates to my heaven were still one hundred percent intact.

My parents have always emphasized the importance of waiting till marriage to have sex—that sex is a holy gift from God meant to be shared by husband and wife. Unlike Gemma, who—let's face it—will not make it to age sixteen without biblical knowledge, I sort of agreed with my mom and dad. I mean, how cool would it be, sometime in the distant future, to marry my true love and know that I'd saved myself for him?

When I discussed this with Gemma, she smirked and asked if my "true love" was supposed to have saved himself for me, too. Like, didn't I want a guy on my wedding night who had some concept of what he was *doing*? Besides, how would I know if my true love and I were sexually compatible if we hadn't done it? What if I waited until *after* I was married, and it turned out my true love had the performance capabilities of our basement sump pump? Then I'd be, like, *stuck*.

Gemma's point was well taken, but it still seemed to me that in specific cases, you could tell whether you'd be sexually compatible with a boy without actually "doing it." Take Sean, for example. We'd known each other since eighth grade and had been boyfriend and girlfriend since just after Christmas. Everything between us pointed to our being sexually compatible if and when the time came. We matched up in so many ways. We cared about our friends, we cared about music, we cared about our families, and we cared about our church lives. We didn't have deep conversations, but hanging out together was easy. For as long as I could remember, my friends had been telling me, "You and Sean Butler would be the best couple," and after we started dating, he told me that his friends had been saying the same thing about me, except in guyspeak.

Here is how Sean first showed romantic interest in me: he showed up at my mom's nondenominational church on Sunday, which, considering that his parents were typical Minnesota Lutherans, meant he had to be highly motivated.

Anyway, I know you'd rather hear about Sean than about my mother. You'd especially like to know whether my theory of prospective sexual compatibility is true in real life. I have to admit that until that night on the puke-ugly rug, I hadn't really been in a position to comment, since the furthest we'd gone had been Sean's hand atop my sweater. Under which had been a tank top, under which had been a bra from Kmart and not from Victoria's Secret, under which had been me.

It's not like part of me hadn't wanted to go further. Most of the time, my body was screaming, "Sean, yes!" while my morals were screaming, "God no!" Every time Sean touched me, my skin was aflame. Okay. That reeks of bad romance novel. But Sean was also sweet, smart, and way cute. And did I mention talented? He sang with a local Christian rock group named Fever. We even wrote songs together.

You might ask: If Sean was so big on Christian values, why was he trying to take off my bra? You might also ask: Why was I about to let him?

I might answer, he made an excellent case for himself when he groaned in my ear, "Who knows when we'll be together again?"

Again, point well taken. The very next day, my family and

I were moving away from Mankato. Yes, this is the twenty-first century and not the twentieth. Yes, there's email, texting, and Skype. But the fact is, I would be there, and Sean would be here, and there would be approximately 1,800 miles between us. The reason I was at the cabin was to attend a going-away party for me.

Which brings me back to the thing about my mother being a minister.

Back when I was fourteen and she was still the minister at our church in Mankato, WMAN-AM radio asked her to fill in one November night for a call-in talk show host who had the flu. My mom was such a success that evening, with her down-home, practical advice—helping callers with everything from sexual problems in their marriages to health crises with aging parents to choosing the best trimmings for a Thanksgiving dinner—that the station offered her a show of her own. They called it *Minister Marsha* and billed her as the anti–Dr. Laura, in that my mom was funny, nonjudgmental, not self-righteous, and didn't intimidate her audience.

Then came the call that changed everything.

My mom was near the end of one show when a kid buzzed in from northern Minnesota. He called himself Dr. Death and said he had a loaded .45 in his lap. He was planning to go downstairs, kill his family, then kill himself. He was on a pre-paid cell phone, so it was impossible to trace the number, and said he was sitting by a window. If the police as much as turned onto his street, he'd go do it.

She used humor, warmth, and insight to talk him down, even telling him about a time when she was fourteen and had been secretly voted the ugliest girl in her class. She only found out when somebody stuck the early-1980s version of a Hot or Not survey in her locker. To make matters worse, the guy she was crushing on *and* her best friend had voted her the ugliest.

Finally, the kid asked my mother to call the closest hospital and have an ambulance come for him. He asked if she would stay on the phone and pray with him, and she did.

A lot of people were listening that night. CNN picked up the story. Then *People* magazine did a piece, and the rest, as they say, is history.

A month later, Mom got the Call from California. I suppose she'd call it the Calling. It was the president of the Church of Beverly Hills—the biggest, richest, most celebrity-packed church in L.A. They were looking for a new minister, and they wanted to meet my mother. A week later, they flew her and my dad to Los Angeles to talk about it.

My parents got the razzle-dazzle treatment. First-class airfare, a bungalow at the Beverly Hills Hotel, and a car and driver for the week. The governor's wife and two members of Congress attended the party in their honor at some supermodel's mansion in the Hollywood Hills. Then, on Sunday morning, Mom preached a guest sermon at the church about the power of prayer, which—my dad reported this, my mother is far too modest—moved the congregation to tears.

By the time they landed back in Minneapolis, she had a firm offer with a salary literally ten times what she was making in Mankato, including a lovely parish home in Beverly Hills, plus a commitment by the church board of directors to get behind her radio show and syndicate it nationally. Since the chairman of Clear Channel was a member of said board, this was not mere hyperbole.

Gemma promised she'd go to church every day for the rest of her natural life if only our mom would accept the job. There was no place she'd rather live than Beverly Hills. Chad was good to go when he found out that the training program for the next Olympics cycle was based at UCLA. Dad, who can write anywhere, declared that while he'd miss our friends, this was a once-in-a-lifetime opportunity and he'd support whatever decision my mother made.

Mom prayed on it for a week. I did, too. Because the only one in our family who was freaking out about utterly, completely, and totally changing our lives was—you guessed it—me. My opinion of Beverly Hills, based on TV shows, was this: Why would I possibly want to live in the land of the plastic and the shallow? Why would my family?

At the end of the week, my parents called a family meeting to make a decision. I presented an excellent case for staying put. It convinced no one. I was outvoted four to one. "Consensus has been reached," my father joked, since there was obviously no consensus.

Let me make two things perfectly clear: First, I did not decide to give it up to Sean that night because I was pissed at the four people who voted against me—namely, my own family, also known as the traitors. Second, let the record reflect I still believe that even if you haven't taken a formal purity oath, having sex with your boyfriend is just plain wrong.

However, in that moment at the lakeside cabin with Sean, right and wrong got a little befuddled as my IQ slipped somewhere south of my navel. I suppose I should say here that it was safe sex, and also, if I'm going to be brutally honest, my reaction was "That's *it*? *That's* what all the shouting is about?" It hurt a little, didn't last very long, and frankly, I liked all the stuff that led up to actual intercourse way better than I liked intercourse.

Afterward, we didn't have much to say to each other. I asked Sean how he felt, and all he could muster was that he loved me. He didn't ask me how I felt, which was kind of sad. On the other hand, I'm not sure I could have offered a coherent answer other than that I was already disappointed in myself—probably not what Sean wanted to hear. I did tell myself that since I was moving to La La Land the very next day, no one would ever know.

In fact, if I wanted, I could act like it had never happened.

Chapter One

Of course, that didn't mean I didn't think about what I'd done with Sean the entire two-hour shuttle van ride from Mankato to Minneapolis–St. Paul International Airport and then a goodly part of the four-hour flight from the Twin Cities to Burbank, California. Fortunately, my father, brother, and sister were sitting in the row behind me, row 12, while I had secured the window seat on the left side of row 11. My father was doing hard-copy revisions of his latest novel, Gemma was rewatching *Jersey Shore* on her iPod, and Chad was sleeping.

As for row 11, unfortunately, the middle and aisle seats were occupied by a pair of adult twin ladies in wide matching poodle-themed skirts. Members of the Poodle Club of America, en route to a poodle convention in Los Angeles, they were traveling with matching champagne toy poodles named Fred and Ginger. Ginger sported a rhinestone collar and her nails were painted silver. Fred had a black tuxedo collar. Their little poodle carriers were a joke.

Some people say that evangelical Christians can get too enthusiastic in their efforts to bring church to the unchurched. I am here to say that they have nothing on the poodle ladies in their efforts to convert me to the pulpit of poodles.

Pretending to sleep was my best option, but then I really did doze off, with thoughts of Sean and what we'd done the night before dancing in my head. Not good. Sugarplums should dance in your head, not the loss of your virginity on the floor at a party and not being too pleased with yourself for having done it.

My mom had come to Los Angeles a week ahead of the rest of us to start at the church; Dad had stayed behind in Mankato so that we kids could finish our finals. The church had put her back in a bungalow at the Beverly Hills Hotel, since our new home was being repainted and re-everything else, but that day it would be ready and we'd all move in. I was half convinced that the moment my mom saw us, she'd know I'd had sex. Sometimes she's spooky like that. If she asked me, I'd be dead, because I found it impossible to lie to her. On the other hand, even if she didn't ask and I didn't tell, it would still be the building of a false impression.

I could imagine her writing a sermon about that.

What woke me up was a poke in my ribs through the space that separated me from one of the poodle ladies. It was Gemma, lifting folds of poodle skirt to find me.

"We're landing!" she shrieked with excitement.

I rubbed my sleepy eyes and then gazed out the window. Thanks to Google Earth, I had an idea of what Los Angeles looks like from five thousand feet, but a computer screen can't give you the scale. It's huge. A hundreds-of-square-miles sprawl of buildings, houses, and freeways, stretching from the San Bernardino Mountains to the ocean. I got a bird's-eye view of the two big freeways, the 101 and the 405, which I would come to know and loathe well. It was just a little after noon—we'd dropped two time zones on the flight—but both freeways were stop and go. Mostly stop.

"Isn't this exciting?" Gemma squealed. "California. Thank you, Mom. Thank you!"

Fifteen minutes later, we were on the ground. I retrieved my guitar from the overhead compartment—it's a beauty, an acoustic Takamine that was an operative result of several hundred hours of babysitting—and slung a small backpack over my other shoulder, and after heartfelt hugs from the poodle ladies, I was good to go. Since it had been eighty degrees in the Twin Cities when we'd taken off, and it was the same temperature here in Burbank, I was traveling comfortably in a battered pair of no-name jeans, a Mankato State University T-shirt, and flip-flops.

The Burbank airport is mercifully small. We'd heard nightmare stories about the big Los Angeles airport, LAX. My dad made a bathroom pit stop and said he wanted to call my mom, so my brother, my sister, and I beat him to baggage claim. It wasn't hard to find the guy from the church who was picking us up. First, he had a hand-lettered sign: WELCOME TO L.A. SHELTON FAMILY. Second, he was the best-looking guy in a room crowded with good-looking people. Easily six foot two, with close-cropped and well-gelled dark hair, he had a cleft chin, broad cheekbones, and blue eyes the color of a clear May sky. He was dressed in hip-casual jeans, a white T-shirt, and a black silk sport coat.

"Whoa!" Gemma whispered. "He's hot!" She did the hair-flip thing she does whenever she approaches a cute boy. This guy, however, was not a cute *boy*. He had to be in his early twenties, at least. I knew the age difference wouldn't bother Gemma a bit.

I waved to the fine guy and he strode over to us with a hand outstretched. "Shelton family! Welcome to Los Angeles. I'm Xan, the church van driver."

"I'm Gemma," my sister purred through her frosty pink lip gloss. "It's *fantastic* to meet you." She held her hand out to him. He took it to shake but she just held on.

Ever so subtly, I kicked her in the shin. She dropped his hand. "I'm Nat." I shook his hand. "And this is our brother, Chad."

"It's great to finally meet you guys," Xan said. "Your mom can't wait to see you." He looked around. "Where's your dad?"

"Pit stop," I explained. "He drank a little too much on the plane. Coffee, that is. Because he doesn't drink much. Alcohol."

I winced, because I knew I sounded like an idiot. I'd always prided myself on not being intimidated by good-looking guys. It wasn't like their looks were something they had earned; they were merely the luck of the genetic lottery. Back in Mankato, Sean was considered a fine guy. But that was Mankato-hot, as opposed to L.A. hot. I looked around baggage claim. There were easily a half dozen guys who would zip past Sean on the Heatometer.

14

"Oh my gosh!" Gemma gasped, staring past me at something.

"Holy shlitz!" Chad added. That was his latest attempt to cuss without actually cussing.

I turned to see the object of their attention. It was Katherine Heigl herself, in black skinny jeans and a couple of layered tank tops, with big sunglasses perched high on her head.

One look at her in person made me realize that the comparison once made between us was almost ridiculously misguided. She was thin. Demoralizingly thin, because I had thought she was one of the few hot young actresses in Hollywood who didn't look like she was a size nothing. But she couldn't have been more than a size four. I felt positively porky. I remembered something I'd read about the camera putting twenty pounds on a person. I felt like Katherine Heigl had just put twenty pounds on me.

Chad's eyes followed longingly as a uniformed flunky arrived to whisk her away. Just then, Dad stepped into the baggage claim area. He broke into a big smile when he saw us with Xan, then trotted over and introduced himself with his usual warmth.

"Do you have any baggage that's coming through?" Xan asked.

My dad shook his head. "All we've got is this carry-on stuff; we shipped everything else." He turned to us. "I couldn't call your mom."

Chad grinned. "Didn't juice your cell?" My father was famous for not turning things off or on: the stove, his cell, the car engine, the water after he brushed his teeth. Some might find it annoying. Fortunately, my mother finds it quirky. She's forgiving that way. But maybe not of her virgin eldest daughter no longer being a virgin.

Geez. Why couldn't I get that out of my head?

I reached into my purse for my cell. "Use my phone, Dad."

"Or we could just surprise her," Chad suggested.

Dad grinned. "That's a great idea."

"Your secret is safe with me," Xan promised as he led us toward the exit. "You're going to love your new house."

"Definitely," Gemma agreed, because Mom had uploaded dozens of photographs. In Mankato, we had a smallish three-bedroom low-slung ranch on a bluff not far from the Blue Earth River. Here the parish home was two stories and half again as big, located on the residential portion of Rodeo Drive north of Santa Monica Boulevard. Gemma would have an actual Rodeo Drive address, and for the first time, she and I would have our own rooms.

"Great. You know Ricardo Montalban used to own it?" Xan asked.

"I didn't, no." My father stroked his chin. "Well, I guess it's not so strange. There are a lot of actors here."

"Who's Ricardo Montalban?" Chad wondered aloud.

Dad grinned. "A big star from before you were born. You're making me feel old."

"You *are* old," Chad pointed out.

We reached the parking structure and then our vehicle, which I expected would be a church van like the one at home. Not. It was a stretch limousine, the kind you see depositing celebrities on the red carpet at the Academy Awards. Discreetly lettered below the blackout glass on the forward passenger door was THE CHURCH OF BEVERLY HILLS. BEVERLY HILLS, CA.

Xan held the door, and Gemma slid into the car as if she'd been doing this sort of thing her entire life, careful to put every inch of her miniskirt-clad legs on display for him. Chad and I clambered in after her.

"The fridge is stocked, and you can use the TV or the CD player," Xan said.

Gemma looked upward. "If this is a dream, please, God, don't let me wake up."

Dad opened the front passenger door and sat next to Xan.

"You don't have to be up here, Mr. Shelton!" Xan exclaimed. "The limo seats twelve."

"Hey, I'd *rather* be up here," Dad assured him.

"Suit yourself, sir." Xan started the car. "Sorry for the walk, but the line at valet parking was insane and I was afraid I'd be late."

Dad ran a hand through his thinning brown hair. "We're not really valet kind of people."

"Speak for yourself," Gemma mumbled.

As we pulled away, I looked out the window at the other cars. Mercedes. BMW. Mercedes. Lexus. Range Rover. Hummer. BMW. BMW. BMW. No wonder American automakers were in such trouble.

As Xan drove, he chatted with my dad. Dad has a gift of being able to talk easily to anybody about pretty much anything. He always says he gets his best material from conversations with new people. I listened in. Xan had come to Los Angeles to be an actor—if he couldn't be an actor, he'd be

17

happy to model—and he lived in the guesthouse of a very famous television producer who was a prominent member of our new church.

Chad opened the fridge, took out a raspberry Arizona iced tea, and put on his iPod—undoubtedly set to Children of Bodom or some other death metal band that he loved. Gemma and I got Fiji water, and then Gemma blasted Pussycat Dolls through the excellent sound system. The Dolls are not, in my opinion, actual music, but I was too busy taking in the scenery to argue with her.

The ride to our new home took us through the heart of Hollywood, and I stared out the smoked glass at the denizens of Sunset and Vine preening for the afternoon. On one corner was a person—man or woman indeterminate—dressed as an alien, holding a picket sign that read THE END IS COMING. Directly behind him was a severely overweight woman of a certain age in an ill-advised string bikini, carrying a sign of her own. It pointed at her ass: THE END.

Gemma was peering out the window, too, at the tourist hustle and bustle, homeless people in rags, and garish neon signs for everything from wax museums to tattoo parlors. "*This is Hollywood?*" she asked rhetorically, sounding like a little kid who had just learned that there was no Santa.

When we stopped at a light, strange people tried to look inside our limo to see what famous person was being chauffeured around. This perked Gemma up considerably. Me? I stared glumly at the unfamiliar landscape. Taco shops next to porn shops next to boutiques. We continued west, through an Asian neighborhood. Then a Russian one. Then a gay one, with the most gorgeous guys walking around who would have no interest in either me *or* Katherine Heigl.

Before I knew it, we were in Beverly Hills. Xan turned onto Rodeo Drive at Wilshire Boulevard, and I was confronted by the designer stores that lined both sides of the street. Gucci. Valentino. Chanel. A single item from one of these stores might cost the entire year's take-home pay of the average person in Mankato.

"Just a couple of minutes now," Xan told us.

"Sam!" Chad exclaimed—his non-cussing version of "damn"—as he stared out at a gorgeous girl in a red Ferrari passing us.

We crossed Santa Monica Boulevard, and Rodeo Drive turned residential, lined by palm trees taller than any building in Mankato. Many houses had gates and hedges to protect the occupants from gawkers, tour buses, and Google Earth Street View. Our house at 427 didn't have a gate. I was glad for that. But I still felt my heart pound as we approached it on the left. 413. 419. 425. 427.

Xan drove right past it.

"You missed our house," Dad pointed out.

Xan looked puzzled, pulled over to the right, and stopped the limo. "No I didn't."

"Yeah, you did," Dad said. "It's 427 North Rodeo Drive. Back up, please."

"You don't live—"

"Back up, please." My dad cut him off, with good reason. Whether I wanted to live here or not, 427 North Rodeo Drive was our new address.

"Okay." Xan shrugged and put the limo in reverse. He backed up and then pulled into the driveway of the house at 427 North Rodeo Drive.

Weird. There was no moving van. Neither of the two cars the movers had brought from Minnesota—our 2002 Subaru Forester and our 2000 Saturn SL2, which I now realized were terribly downscale for Los Angeles—was parked in the driveway. There was nothing in the driveway, in fact, but a single bright yellow Gold Star Pest Control van and two workmen spreading gold tarpaulins on the front lawn.

Chad took out his earbuds. "What's up with this?"

Dad looked mystified. "You took the words right out of my mouth."

Xan looked confused. "Mr. Shelton? I asked you if you knew about the Montalban house—"

"Right. This house," Dad said.

Xan rubbed the deep cleft in his chin. "No. Not this house. This is the parish house. Not the Montalban house. You didn't talk to your wife before you took off?"

"Why? It would have been five in the morning here," I pointed out.

"Ah. Right," Xan said. "A little misunderstanding. Let me take you to where you're actually living."

My father looked at me. "Nat? Call your mother."

I did. But by the time I reached her—she didn't answer, so I sent her a text and it took a few minutes for her to ring back—Xan had driven us up into the neighborhood above the Beverly Hills Hotel. In fact, when my cell rang, he'd just stopped at a white wrought-iron gate to enter an access code.

"Mom? We're here." The gate swung open, and we started up a long secluded driveway.

"You're here?" she exclaimed. "I'm not. I'm at the hardware store, but heading home. I can't wait to see you guys. Why didn't you call when you—"

The call dropped, which wasn't such a bad thing, because I was too busy staring at the structure now coming into view to pay close attention to my mother.

"Movie companies rent this place for location shoots," Xan explained as he stopped the limo. "Ten grand a day, fully furnished. Your own furniture is in storage. I hope you don't mind. When they found termites at the parish house on Rodeo Drive, the board had to scramble. One of the members owns the place."

I looked at my brother and sister. They were clearly in as much shock as I was.

We got out. In front of us was a three-story gleaming white mansion, easily ten times the size of the place on Rodeo Drive. One end of the driveway was big enough to hold fifteen or twenty cars and paved not with black asphalt, but with red brick that made me think of Mexico. The home itself was massive, all blocks and right angles, with a white brick walkway that led to a double mahogany front door.

"Um, there aren't any windows," Gemma noted.

"Not in front," Xan said. "The architect wanted it that way. Wait till you get around the back. You can see everything. The city, the mountains, the ocean. The view is killer."

To our surprise, the front door opened. An extremely tan woman with a precise blond bob and a thin figure stepped out.

Behind her were three teenagers. There were two girls about my age, equally thin and blond. One was tall, with those thick straight-across eyebrow-brushing bangs that look great on some people but make other people's heads look like bowling balls. She was in the non–bowling ball group. She wore a pink and white floral sundress and sandals. The other girl was round-faced and petite under her layered camis and white shorts. The third teenager was a guy with short rust-colored hair and a wide grin. My guess? He was around Chad's age. Which meant that Chad looked like the guy's babysitter.

"Welcome!" the lady shouted. "You must be the rest of the Sheltons! Welcome to Los Angeles. Come in, come in! I'm Connie Kay from church, and these are three members of our youth group, Sandra, Lisa, and Trevor. We're sort of your unofficial welcoming committee. Let us show you around your new home!"

My dad shook Connie's French-manicured hand. "Thank you. But . . . this is just temporary. Till the termite problem gets fixed. Right?"

Connie shrugged cheerfully.

"Because it's very . . . opulent for a minister's family," he added. "Not that we don't appreciate it."

"Actually, we *love* it," Gemma gushed.

"You'll love it even more when you see the inside," Sandra, the taller of the two girls, said. "Time for your tour! And welcome."

I, Natalie Shelton of Mankato, Minnesota, was about to step into my very own *Cribs*.

22

Chapter Two

I turned when I heard the familiar sound of our Saturn's dicey muffler. My mother was back. I was so glad to see her that I temporarily forgot about Connie, her teen minions, and my transgression of biblical proportions that had taken place the night before.

I ran to her as she got out of the car. So did the rest of the family. There were actually tears on my dad's cheeks. Aww. They'd only been separated a week. It made me realize that this whole moving thing had to be tough on him, no matter how often he said he supported my mom's decision. He had as many friends out here as I did. Which is to say none.

We shared a group hug, which might have been smarmy in any other circumstances but at that moment felt just right.

"That welcome does not mean you can bring home Cs on your report card," my mom teased when we broke apart. Then, spotting the welcoming committee, she turned all business.

"Come on, everyone. These good people have been waiting an hour for you. Come say hello." She winked at me. "I think you're going to like your room."

Ten minutes later, Xan had quietly taken his leave, Gemma was with Lisa, Trevor was with Chad, my parents were with Connie, and I was being shown through my new abode by Sandra. Yes, it was big. Yes, it was spectacular. Connie had said, and I quote, "It's a masterpiece of cubistic forms and volumes that are framed by head-on city, canyon, and ocean views. It reflects a spirited interplay of space, color, and light that is typical of the architect's work. The architect, Ricardo Legorreta, tried to pull in elements of Picasso, Mexico, and the natural beauty of Southern California. It's really quite spectacular."

As we say in Minnesota, you betcha.

Anyway, Sandra took me on the grand tour. Even as I came to know her, like her, and realize that she and I might become friends, I decided I hated the house.

We entered via a long brick walkway, with a lattice fence to our right and several big cactuses beyond that. A series of concrete boxes delineated one side of the walkway and kept people from wandering down a hillside that dropped steeply. The mahogany doors opened to a stark downstairs interior, with very little furniture, a few mirrors, and blindingly white walls with tops that angled rather niftily instead of meeting the ceiling. There was a burnt-sienna parquet wood floor and two huge picture windows that looked out toward the ocean ten miles away.

"Look at this living room!" Sandra gushed as she brought me to it. "You can see the Pacific from the windows!"

The view was, admittedly, striking. The problem was, for a living room, you really couldn't do much living in it. Looking Lilliputian in the middle of all this open space were two white leather couches that faced each other, with a mosaic coffee table in between that held several pieces of southwestern folk art. The table sat on an intricately designed handwoven rug.

"Nice, don't you think?" Sandra prompted me. "You really get fooled, because even though there are no windows in front, there are tons of them in back. Nice!" She was obviously eager to please.

"Nice," I echoed politely. This room looked like it belonged in the design wing of a modern-art museum in New York City. If you put your feet up on those couches, it was probably a Class C felony.

The mansion went on and on. Formal dining room with a table that sat twenty. Enormous state-of-the-art kitchen, which I knew my father, who did a lot of the cooking, would go crazy over. The kitchen opened to a patio of white and grass green marble, with comfy outdoor furniture and a massive fire pit. Off the patio were a hot tub and a swimmer's continuous-action wave pool that would make Chad drool.

We went back inside and explored the rest of the downstairs. There were two bedrooms, one of which was my parents' master suite. One whole wall was a window, and a gigantic bed faced the view. I've heard that California has a mattress named after it, the California king, which looks like two regular king-size beds put together. This was a king-size king. Their bedroom had a black and white theme; the bed was draped with a luxurious damask patterned comforter that went down to the floor. There were a tall black armoire and two white leather button-tufted lounge chairs that sat in front of a fireplace. Above the fireplace was a gigantic flat-screen TV. Their bathroom was all white marble and had a Jacuzzi tub that could hold half of Mankato. Off the bathroom were two enormous walk-in closets, one for my mom, one for my dad. My parents' clothes were already unpacked into just one of the closets. Maybe they'd rent out the other one.

"Your bedrooms are upstairs," Sandra told me. "Come on, I'll show you."

We mounted a spectacular spiral staircase and found ourselves deposited in a sitting area with a dove gray suede couch and matching low-slung chairs, a wall-mounted TV, silver metallic cushions on the floor, and even a small refrigerator and wet bar. I felt my sandals sink into the plush white rug. All I could think was, what if I wanted to eat chips and a bowl of salsa while watching TV? What if I dropped a big-ass chunk of salsa on that rug? I was pretty sure an alarm would go off and the interior design police would cart me away.

"Your bedroom's the one on the left," Sandra said eagerly as she opened yet another mahogany door. "You're going to love it."

I stepped inside. Whoa. Back in Mankato, Gemma and I had shared a room forever. We'd had bunk beds, a couple of desks from Ikea in Minneapolis, ditto Ikea dressers, and very little floor space. There were two small windows and a bulletin board covered haphazardly with photos and souvenirs from Gemma's life. She was in almost every photo—no shocker there. Over my bed was a framed poster from the movie *Once*, about a guy and a girl who come together to make the most moving music ever without doing something cliché like falling in love. I've seen that film at least a dozen times.

My new bedroom looked like a penthouse suite at the nicest hotel in the world, with a view of the Hollywood Hills through a picture window. There was a four-poster bed with an airy canopy of sheer textured ivory cotton gauze across the top and a billowy hand-knotted white comforter that fell in graceful pleated folds to the gleaming, polished hardwood floor, which was dotted with intricately woven rugs. The closet— okay, I admit I was psyched about this one—was practically the size of my high school's football stadium. There was an amazing closet-organizing system, which included a center rack that rotated at the push of a button. The movers had already unpacked my stuff and hung it up. It took up, oh, say, a hundredth of the space. Less, actually.

"I kinda poked around a little before you got here," Sandra admitted. "You can cover the window like this. The glass on your windows adjusts to the light, but you can also adjust it yourself." She pointed to a discreet button on the wall near the window, then sat on the edge of the—*my*—bed. "I have to tell you, Nat—can I call you Nat?"

"Sure," I said, feeling a bit overwhelmed.

"The whole church has been so excited about your family. And when my friends and I found out that you were our age, we were so psyched." She grinned at me and looped some wheat-colored hair behind one ear. "I guess what I'm trying to say is, we're just really glad you're here."

I couldn't help smiling back. It's always nice to feel

wanted. Still, I couldn't get over my Alice-through-the-looking-glass feeling. I mean, yes, Sandra was being really nice. And my new bedroom was amazing. But like the living room—and the entire house, for that matter—it just didn't feel like me. The only things that made me feel better were that my bed had been made with my Minnesota sheets, blankets, and pillows and that my guitar—I'd forgotten all about it, maybe Xan had brought it up—was leaning against the wall to the left of a hand-painted nightstand. I moved to it, looking for something that would connect the "me" of here to the "me" of there—back home in Minnesota, where I belonged.

"You play guitar," Sandra observed.

I sat on a white chaise lounge near the picture window. "A little." I opened the case. It smelled of my room in Mankato. I felt a lump swell in my throat.

"There are a lot of places to play here in L.A.," Sandra said. "Do you perform?"

"Once in a while." I strummed idly. An E-minor chord. A G. And then the chord progression of one of my favorite songs of all time, Leonard Cohen's "Hallelujah." I closed my eyes and started to sing the first verse, about how King David wrote music that pleased God so much.

To my surprise, Sandra joined in. Even more surprising, she had a lovely voice—an alto to my soprano. I kept my eyes closed, but we sang the whole song. She knew the lyrics as well as I did. We even did some impromptu harmonizing on the chorus.

When it was over, I strummed one last chord, let it dissipate, and finally opened my eyes. We shared a smile.

"That was beautiful. Where did you learn to sing like that? Are you in the choir?" I asked.

She grinned. "You know Nona?"

"Sure." Nona was one of the truly groundbreaking female singers of the 1980s and 1990s. These days, she'd shifted her focus from rock to musical theater, having written and starred in a Christian rock opera about Joseph and Mary.

"She belongs to our church," Sandra explained. "Which means you'll meet her. Actually, she's my mother."

Whoa baby. Sandra was Nona's daughter? No wonder she had such a good voice.

"If you want to meet her, come over later," Sandra offered. "I know she'd love to get to know you. We know what it's like to move to L.A. from another place. I moved here, too."

I'd had no idea. "From where?"

"Manhattan." Sandra brushed some of her flaxen hair off her face. "We had a townhouse on the Upper East Side. I lived there my whole life, and it broke my heart to move away. That was after sixth grade. But my dad died—he was a lot older than my mom—and she couldn't deal with going to the same restaurants and the same church, walking on the same streets she used to with him." She shrugged. "We came out here for a new start."

I put my guitar down, thinking that I would never have guessed that about Sandra. Huh. Maybe she really could be my friend.

We went into the upstairs den, cracked open a couple of Cokes that were already cooling in the fridge—the welcoming committee must have stocked the place, which was amazingly thoughtful—and talked some more. We would both be going to Beverly Hills High School in the fall. We both liked Will Ferrell, hated *Gossip Girl,* and had started the Twilight series in ninth grade. We didn't drink, smoke, or do drugs, though Sandra warned me that 90 percent of the kids out here were happy to do all three, and often at the same time.

"It's easy to get sucked into the whole teen party scene," she said. "I mean, girls out here? If they haven't had sex by the time they're fourteen, they lie and say they have, to be cool. It's just so easy to get corrupted."

"It won't happen with me," I assured her. "That's not my style."

Oh yeah? a little voice inside me piped up. *Having sex with Sean last night wasn't your style, either.*

That was different, I told the voice.

Yeah, the voice shot back. *That was worse.*

Fortunately, right then I heard a squeal followed by laughter. Gemma and Lisa seemed to be getting along like they'd grown up together in the same designer playpen. Lisa was giving my sister a rundown of who was hot and who was not at our church. Trevor and Chad came in and raided the cupboards. They left with armfuls of junk food, babbling about the Xbox 360 in Chad's new room. Evidently, it had enough games to make any thirteen-year-old boy think the Rapture was upon us. By the looks of it, they were anticipating a long stay post-tribulation.

Before I knew it, an hour had passed. Remarkably, without any planning, I'd made my first friend in L.A. Even better, it looked like Gemma and Chad had made friends, too. Hey, once a big sister, always a big sister. You look out for your siblings whether you want to or not. It just comes naturally.

Sandra was talking about the church youth group—she was incoming president—and an upcoming volunteer project later in the summer when her iPhone rang. I recognized the melody. "Manhattan Morning." By her mother.

"My mom," she explained as she glanced at her iPhone.

I nodded.

She sprang up. "Whoa. I'm super-late. We're going to this screening later. It's the new Spielberg. The one that comes out in August?" She frowned. "I'd invite you, but we had to RSVP ahead of time. But next time?"

"I'd like that."

A screening of a new Steven Spielberg movie? That didn't happen in Mankato. Ever. I really *would* like that.

Then she smacked herself in the head. "I am such an idiot! I almost forgot."

"Forgot what?"

"Follow me." She led me back into my room, knelt down, and reached under my bed.

"We knew you played guitar," she admitted. "So the church youth group got you a present."

There, before my disbelieving eyes, she extracted a guitar case that looked a lot like Eric Clapton's crocodile model, except this one was zebra-striped. It was obviously leather—unlike my own—and it was obviously expensive.

Then she opened the case. Slack-jaw time, again.

"We asked your mom if you had a twelve string," Sandra explained. "She said no." She smiled and handed me the guitar.

Unbelievable. I was holding in my hand a Breedlove Classic XII acoustic that I knew had to have cost more than three thousand dollars. It made my gorgeous Takamine look cheap by comparison.

I shook my head. "I can't accept this."

"You already did," Sandra said breezily. "It's a present from the youth group. And you don't want us to hate you, do you?" She grinned again. "So, go for it."

What could I do? I played a tune I'd written for Sean called "This Guy." I didn't sing; I just played the melody. It sounded like it was being played on a three-thousand-dollar guitar. Because it was.

Sandra applauded when I was done. "I know who's entertaining on our next retreat."

"Yeah," I said, laughing. "You." I carefully put the guitar back in its case. "I know you have to go, but come downstairs first. I want you to meet my parents."

I felt pretty good as I led Sandra to the lower level, but the house was so big that I had to text my dad to find out where they were. It turned out they were on the back patio, with a dozen other church members Connie had invited for a meet-and-greet barbecue, conducted by a very tall African American chef looking even taller in an enormous chef's hat.

Sandra greeted my parents warmly and thanked my mom for being a coconspirator in the purchase of my new guitar.

"Happy to help." Mom looped a slender arm around my shoulders. "Now, make sure you guys do three thousand dollars' worth of charity work together."

"We will," Sandra promised. "We've got an interfaith soup kitchen project in the Valley in a couple of weeks."

"I'm in," I declared.

"Sweet," Sandra replied. "Come on. Walk me to my car."

I did; we hugged each other goodbye, then Sandra got in her gray Prius and drove down the majestic brick driveway. I watched until her car was out of sight.

So far so good, I thought. I was psyched that I had made my first friend. I headed back to the house, trying to decide what I wanted to do. Did I want to hang out on the patio? Work on "The Shape I'm In," my latest song? Or call Sean? There was so much to talk about, if he was willing to talk.

I tried Sean. No answer, got his voice mail, which was a letdown. I left a brief message, telling him I was okay and asking him to call me later. But not too late, since I was sure I'd be crashing early. Non-call out of the way, I knew what I wanted to do. Play my really incredible twelve string and see if I could come up with a melody for the new tune.

I practically ran through the house and up the stairs to my room.

I opened the door and screamed.

Sitting on my bed, with my new guitar in his hands, was a very hot—and did I mention buff?—guy.

He was also very naked, except for a heavy chain wrapped around his right ankle.

"Hey." He greeted me as if we were long-lost naked friends. He strummed a few chords expertly. "Insane guitar." He strummed another chord. "I'm Shepard. What's your name?"

Chapter Three

"Get out of my room!" I shrieked, trying hard to look everywhere except at a certain part of his anatomy.

"Don't be like that," he chided gently. "I'm really good."

I could feel my face turn the color of marinara sauce. "I don't care how good you are! I just, just . . . ," I blustered.

"I meant on the *guitar*, babe. Watch." He played an amazing lick.

I was pretty sure that if I ever wrote a memoir, finding Buff Naked Guy in my bedroom, on my bed, playing my guitar like a rock god, would be right up there in the chapter of memorable experiences. However, Buff Naked Guy Who Sounded Like a Rock God was clearly insane. Which meant, just as clearly, I had to hustle downstairs to tell my parents. But as I pivoted to make my getaway, he ripped another smoking riff out of my guitar, using one finger instead of a guitar pick, the notes rolling and building and filling my room. It was as intricate as a Bach fugue but with the driving intensity of

Metallica. I don't know a lot of things, but I do know music. I couldn't help it: that riff stopped me in my tracks.

I turned back and saw him tilt his head toward the ceiling as he played and shout at the heavens above. "Randy Rhoads? You listening, dude? You suck!"

Randy Rhoads. Used to play with Ozzy Osbourne. Dead. Possibly in the heavens above. In fact, probably, since he died in a plane crash and didn't use a lot of drugs or alcohol. It meant Buff Naked Guy Etc., even if he was certifiable, was shouting in the right direction.

Enough was enough. I left and headed down to the backyard barbecue and my parents. *There's a naked guy playing lead on my bed,* I practiced mentally. Yeah, that ought to get their attention.

The barbecue area was empty. Crap. Why did this place have to be so huge? I found my folks at the front door, waving as the last of their guests departed, my dad's arms around my mom.

"Nice welcome," he said to her.

She nodded her agreement. "I always say, you can find good people everywhere."

"I totally agree," I chimed in. "For example, at this very moment, there's a nice guy in my bedroom playing my guitar. Did I mention that he's naked?"

Up went my dad's eyebrows. "A naked guy," he repeated. "And he's playing your guitar. That's all?" My father obviously wanted more confirmation.

"So far," I said. I folded my arms in what I hoped was a definitive gesture.

"Charlie, maybe you'd better go see what's going on," my

mother advised him. "Perhaps one of our guests had one too many beers."

"Perhaps," my dad agreed.

I couldn't believe how calm they were. "He's too young to be your guest and too old to be mine," I said.

Funny how I wasn't totally freaking out, either. Maybe it was because the guy was so hot—forgive me my moment of shallowness, God, thank you. Maybe it was because the guy was so talented. Or maybe it was because in his current state of undress, there was zero chance that he was carrying a concealed weapon.

"Nat, wait here," my dad instructed, and he and my mom headed upstairs. Just as I was contemplating following them, our doorbell sounded. Huh. No one had buzzed from the gate down the hill. Probably one of the guests had forgotten something.

I opened the heavy door. A girl my age stood there. She had lush mahogany hair that fell in artfully tousled waves to her shoulders. Her eyes were the color of the sky at thirty thousand feet, and she had Angelina-worthy pouty lips. She was both curvy and skinny, in a white ribbed tank top, tiny cutoff jeans, and flip-flops. She had some kind of super PDA in her hands, and a shoulder bag.

"Hi," she said, her voice worried. "You just moved in, right? I saw the moving truck this morning. I'm Alexis Samuels. We live back there." She gestured vaguely toward the canyon.

"Natalie Shelton." I held out a hand and she shook it. "Call me Nat," I added.

"And call me Alex. So listen, I think my brother, Shep, is

here." She held up the PDA. "At least, that's what my tracker says."

Suddenly, it all made sense. The ankle bracelet on Buff Naked Guy Etc.'s right ankle. If what the girl was holding was a GPS tracking device, that ankle bracelet had to be a transmitter. I saw no reason to doubt her.

"He's in my room playing my guitar," I said. "I just saw him."

She winced. "And he's wearing . . . ?"

I leaned against the wall. "Adam? Eve? The garden before the whole apple thing?"

"Playing guitar and getting naked are two of his favorite things to do," Alex said. "All the others are illegal." She sighed and raked a hand through her glorious hair. "I'm really sorry. He's allegedly under house arrest. Drug charges. If it makes you feel any better, he's totally harmless. He's never hurt anyone except himself."

"Because he's still using," I said, filling in the blanks.

"Yeah." She shook her head ruefully. "It sucks and I've tried so hard to—" She stopped midsentence and held up one of those oversized purses that girls in L.A. carry around— the ones that cost four figures and look like you could fit your entire family inside. "Clothes for him."

She looked so upset that I reached out and touched her arm. "You're a good sister."

"If you knew me better, you probably wouldn't say that." She shifted the oversized purse to her other hand. "You can't imagine the places I've found him—Runyon Canyon Park, people's houses—stark naked, playing his guitar or someone else's he happened to find. Sometimes by the time I get there, he's already asleep. So far, no one's called the cops. But it's just a matter of time."

"My parents went upstairs to investigate. Come on, I'll show you." I opened the door wider. Her Geiger counter thing beeped more loudly.

She stepped into the palatial entranceway. "I really want to thank you for helping me. Sometimes people aren't so . . . compassionate."

"Well, as my mom would say, everyone has their demons."

"Your mother sounds like a saint," Alex said.

"Close enough. She's a minister."

I led her upstairs and the GPS device beeped like a hamster in heat. We found my parents coming out of my room. I quickly introduced them to Alex and filled them in.

"Your brother's out like a light," my father said. He cracked open my door so that we could peer in.

Sure enough, Shepard was fast asleep, snoring on my bed, covered by the sheets and the white comforter. I made a mental note to find our new home's washing machine as soon as he was gone.

"Where're Gemma and Chad?" I asked, concerned that my younger sibs might be freaked by all of this.

"Out at the pool," Dad assured me.

Mom nodded. "No worries."

This might be the moment for me to pause and say that I have really nice parents.

"So, what do we do now?" I asked.

"I can take it from here," Alex said. "Thank you all, really. For being so kind."

My mother gently touched Alex's arm. Funny. It was the same gesture I'd made toward her downstairs. "We'll wait in the den."

"Sure you don't need us?" my father asked.

Alex shook her head. "Trust me. I'm used to this."

Apparently, it was true. My parents and I only had to wait about ten minutes—we amused ourselves by watching the Weather Channel's ten-day forecast for Southern California, which promised day after day after day after day of clear sunny skies and temperatures in the mid-eighties—before my bedroom door opened and Alex led her brother out of my room. He was now dressed in faded jeans and a white T-shirt. I willed myself to look everyplace except at . . . *you know*. I mean, having seen his—*you know*—and now seeing the outline of his *you know* through the jeans.

Alex made the awkward introductions. "Well, I feel as if I know you already," Shep quipped with a smile that showed off Chiclet white teeth. "Thank you for the hospitality." He bowed gallantly. "And I'm sorry to have disturbed you."

"I'm guessing you're wearing that ankle cuff for a reason," Mom said.

Shep nodded.

"If we had little kids, I'd be a lot more upset than I am right now." Dad's voice was stern. "You need to be more responsible for your behavior."

"He's working on it," Alex said quickly. Somehow, I had the feeling that she was used to defending her big brother.

"Because next time—fair warning—I will call the cops," my dad added.

39

Shep nodded. "Fair warning," he echoed. "By the way, whose guitar is the twelve string?"

I waggled my fingers in the air.

"Fantastic instrument," he said.

Fantastic instrument. Obviously he was talking about the guitar. But it made me think about his *you know* again, and I swear if I hadn't been intimately engaged with Sean's *you know* the night before, I would not have kept obsessing in this direction.

"I'd be happy to show you a few tricks sometime," Shep added. "If you're interested."

I opened my mouth to speak, but my father beat me to it. "Thanks, but I'd rather not have you teaching my daughter any 'tricks.'"

I could feel myself blushing again. "He didn't mean—"

"I think I'd better get my brother home now," Alex interrupted. "Nat, want to walk us back?"

It had been a long day that had started in Mankato and ended in this movie-set mansion in the Bel Air hills, but I would be lying if I didn't say I was flying at Alex's invite. Back in Minnesota, I had a lot of friends—Shelby was the best of them, but it wasn't like we were soul sisters—most of whom I'd grown up with. One of my worries was having to make all new friends. Yet I'd been here for just a few hours and had already made a new friend in Sandra. Now there was Alex, too. In Mankato, a lot of my friends were also friends with each other. Maybe Sandra and Alex already were friends. It was possible.

I turned to my parents. "Anything I need to be home for?"

Mom shook her head. "Have fun." She bumped a hip into

40

my dad's side. "What do you say we change into bathing suits and join the kids in the pool, handsome?"

Once we were outside, Alex showed me a very cool short-cut to her house, which involved a you-wouldn't-know-it-was-there-unless-someone-showed-you footpath that started about halfway down our driveway, a short jaunt downhill to a dry streambed, a walk north in this streambed with scrub brush and cooing pheasants all around us, past one huge brown mansion high on the hill, and then a hike uphill to a trail similar to the one we'd descended at my new place. We emerged on Alex's back patio—roughly half the size of a football field, with a guitar-shaped swimming pool, a tennis court, a paddle-tennis court, and a hot tub. All the way, Shepard was normal as normal could be. I learned that until his arrest, he'd been the lead guitarist of Bruiser, a death metal band in the vein of Lamb of God. Not a band I adored, but Chad was crazy about them. Wait till he heard that their former lead guitarist had paid an unannounced visit to our new house, and my bed. As we walked through the ravine, Shep regaled me with stories of Bruiser's recent tour of Japan, including a visit with the country's foreign minister. Then, once we got to Alex's deck, he excused himself with another thank-you to me and my parents for our help and went inside.

"Let's sit for a while, okay? You good?" Alex asked as she plopped down in a comfortable-looking wicker chair. I sat in the one next to hers. "Want something to drink? Iced tea?"

"Okay. Sure."

"Great." There was a steel and glass table a few feet away with a white telephone on it. She called the house kitchen and asked for a fruit tray, a plate of biscotti, a pitcher of iced tea, and two glasses of Fiji water. Then she thanked whomever had answered and came back.

"We have a great house staff. Mrs. Cleveland? The cook? She used to work for Platinum. You know, the singer?"

"I think I read that she's in rehab again," I mused.

"Yeah, she and Shep had a thing. Of course, she and *everyone* have had a thing." Alex closed her eyes and raised her face to the setting sun. "Anyway, we were lucky to get her. Miguel—he's the houseman—will bring everything out in a minute."

Whoa baby. Alex's family had a cook? And a houseman, which I assumed was the moral equivalent of a butler? What else did they have? Drivers? Gardeners? Housekeepers? Massage therapists who came to the house after breakfast and dinner? It was all so new to me. Back in Minnesota, no matter how busy my parents were, or how busy we kids were, we cooked, cleaned, and kept up the house by ourselves. We'd never, ever had a housekeeper or a nanny or any other kind of help.

"Your parents must be really busy if you have a cook and a houseman," I commented.

"My parents are dead. Northern Air flight 504? They were on it. It's just us. Shepard, me, and my sister, Chloe."

My insides squeezed. I remembered Northern Air 504. It had gone down in heavy weather on approach to Honolulu three or four years earlier. The investigation blamed wind shear. The passengers and crew—more than 155 people in all—were killed.

"I'm so sorry." My voice actually cracked on the word "sorry."

"Yeah. Me too. But life goes on."

I raised my knees to my chin and wrapped my arms around them. "How old is Chloe?"

"Eight. She's away at camp for the summer, and then she'll head back to boarding school. Which bites, if you ask me. But my brother has legal custody of us both. Which means he decides. I'm sort of along for the ride. Until I'm eighteen, that is. Then, we'll see. At least money isn't a problem. My folks had a lot of life insurance, and Shep made a ton of money when he was touring. But still . . ."

"Being raised by your brother? That has to be hard."

I hated myself for saying that. It sounded like such a platitude, because it was. Somehow, though, it didn't matter. Either Alex had been looking to talk to someone for a long time, or it was my having the-face-everyone-wants-to-spill-everything-to. Or both. Whatever it was, Alex talked, even as white-jacketed Miguel—a striking man in his forties with one of the best handlebar mustaches I've ever seen not in a movie—came silently onto the patio, set up our refreshments on the table, and left so quickly we didn't even have time to say thank you.

She talked about her parents. How much she missed them. How hard it was to have Shepard as her guardian—and how dicey it was with Shep being busted for drugs. She'd been very close with her father, who had been a CEO with one of the biggest record labels in town. Her sister, Chloe, had been super-close with their mother, who had been a city attorney and very active in local politics. In so many ways, Alex felt adrift.

"But . . . you must have a lot of friends," I ventured.

"Sure." She smiled wearily. "I'll introduce you around. Tomorrow night a bunch of us are going to the movies at the cemetery. Maybe you want to come?"

"Movies at the cemetery?" I was baffled.

She explained that at the Hollywood Forever Cemetery in Hollywood, there were free movies during the summer; people came with blankets, chairs, and picnics. "I think tomorrow night is *Sleepless in Seattle*. It'll be fun."

I grinned. "I'd love to."

"If you have any friends you want to invite . . . ," she began. "But I guess not. You just got here."

I sat up straighter in the chair. This was working out perfectly. "I do, actually. Have a friend here, I mean."

"Cool, invite her." Alex stood. "I'm going to the bathroom in the cabana. Call your friend if you want."

As she walked off, I slipped my cell from my pocket and dialed Sandra.

"Sandra?" I began when she answered. "It's Nat . . . Natalie . . . Shelton. The new minister's—"

"Oh, hi and shut up!" she ordered jokingly. "I already feel like I've known you forever."

A little bubble of happiness welled up inside me. "That's such a sweet thing to say," I told her.

"You know how it is," she went on. "Sometimes you just click with a person. So what's up?"

"I met one of my neighbors, and she invited me to come with her and her friends tomorrow to this cemetery to see a movie—"

"Hollywood Forever," Sandra interjected.

"That's it," I replied. "And she asked if there was anyone I wanted to invite, so I thought of you, and, well, I'm calling."

"Sweet," Sandra said. "I love that place."

"Can you come?"

"I don't see any reason why not. By the way, who's the neighbor? Someone from church?"

"I don't know where she goes to church—or even *if* she goes," I admitted. "Her name is Alexis. Alex Samuels."

Dead silence. I mean, really, really dead silence. So dead I thought I'd lost the call until I checked my cell and saw we were still connected.

"Sandra, are you there?"

More silence. Then: "Yeah. I'm here." Her voice was hard. "Natalie, I'm going to say this once, and only because you're new and have no way of knowing."

I had no idea what she was talking about. "Knowing what?"

"This," Sandra went on, her voice steely ice. "If you know what's good for you, stay far away from Alex Samuels."

Chapter Four

That night, as I lay in bed thinking back on the strangest twenty-four hours of my life, Sandra's words on the phone came to me again and again. "If you know what's good for you, stay far away from Alex Samuels."

What the heck was *that* about? Whatever it was, wasn't Sandra being a tad melodramatic? Maybe living in La La Land just did that to a person after a while. I'd asked Sandra to tell me more, but she'd said something about how Christian girls don't gossip, which I know for a fact is utter baloney. Gossiping is an equal opportunity character flaw.

When Alex came back, I told her that my friend was busy and couldn't come to the movie, which was pretty much the truth, in a way.

For the next hour, before I got so tired I was ready to go home, I was two people with her. Person One was the girl truly interested in everything Alex had to say. As usual, like in the ladies' room, she mostly talked and I mostly listened. Of course, her life was a heck of a lot more glamorous than my life. She'd visited forty countries. I don't know if I've visited forty *counties*. She'd been to every great restaurant in Los Angeles and half the great restaurants in California. My dining experience in Mankato was pretty much limited to the same places you could go anywhere in the country, places that ended with an apostrophe *s*. Applebee's. Denny's. Like that. She'd dropped the names of designer boutiques she liked to shop—Alaïa, Kitson, Intermix—the way my friends and I talked about Target or Old Navy.

Person Two, on the other hand, was watching and listening to Person One talking to Alex, trying to figure out why Sandra had warned me to stay away from her. I thought I had pretty good radar about people. For the life of me, I couldn't figure out why I ought to run in the other direction. Besides, I'm not the kind of person who lets other people tell her who she should or should not be friends with. I liked Alex. I was the new girl, in a new place, and was happy to have a new friend.

Then there was a bonus. Just before I went home, Shepard came down with a couple of Gibson acoustic guitars. As wigged out as he'd been in my room, he now seemed normal. He handed me one of the guitars—Alex said that when musical ability had been given out, she had been at the back of the line—and I got to jam with the best guitarist I've ever met. It was simple twelve-bar blues; I played rhythm and he played lead. For one golden sequence, though, at Shepard's urging (and through my intense discomfort, by the way), I took the lead while he switched to rhythm. I protested, but Alex egged me on.

So I played. It was glorious. Jamming with Shepard Samuels out on an open-air deck in the Los Angeles hills, the sun starting to set over the Santa Monica Mountains and the Pacific beyond. I'm not going to say that it changed my mind about the move. I still wanted to get on the next plane back to Minnesota. But it sure made the ending of the first day different from the beginning.

My parents were already in bed when I came home from Alex's, so I went up to my room. I got an email from Sean at ten o'clock, just before I went to sleep for the first time in my new house, with "Sorry I Missed Your Calls" in the subject line. It wasn't very long, just saying he hoped that the day had been okay, that the new place was homey, and that he and I were still good now that we had done it. Not a word about how he felt, and not a question about how I felt, though there was something about God forgiving. I skimmed over that part really quickly, because I didn't think God had much to do with the night before.

Sean went on for a few lines about his day, shockingly ordinary in comparison to my own. He had a summer job as a custodial assistant at the Mankato Mall, where he spent his days on his hands and knees scraping gum off the tile floor. He said that if I wanted to IM him, he'd be online for a while.

I checked to see if he was still online. He wasn't, which wasn't so bad. My day had started at five a.m. when you take into account the change of time zone. I wouldn't have been much good in a chat, and if we turned on our webcams, he would have seen me yawn every three minutes. Not so attractive. So I emailed him back with a brief but newsy summary of my day, said we'd definitely talk the next day, then clicked off.

I still wasn't sure what I wanted to say about what had happened at the cabin. He'd written that he hoped he and I were still good. We were. But guilty as I was, I didn't know if I had the guts to tell him how I'd felt about the experience, or even how uncertain my feelings were. As for Sean, I couldn't imagine him getting emotional about the subject at all.

That made me think about how we had been communicating lately. How we rarely talked about big stuff. How our conversations were always safe. I tried to remember the last really deep conversation we'd had, or the last real argument. I couldn't.

I got in the glass-enclosed brown and white marble shower, which could be turned into a steam room with the flick of a switch. There was also a marble bathtub with Jacuzzi jets in case I was pining for that in-home spa experience. The toilet was in its own separate little room, and there was a phone on the wall next to it. Then there was the vanity, in yet another connecting room, with a long marble counter with built-in cubbyholes and drawers in which to put my pathetically small collection of drugstore cosmetics. Mirrors covered one wall, and two of the mirrors pulled away from the wall so you could get a 270-degree view of yourself, which is either intensely cool or intensely intimidating. For me, it was intensely intimidating.

After drying off in this luxurious bathroom with the same ordinary green towels I used at home in Minnesota—talk about a clash of cultures!—I thought about working on the lyrics to "The Shape I'm In," but instead went to bed.

As a rule, I am a bad sleeper. Odd, I know. It takes me a long time to fall asleep, and I have some weird sleeping quirks, like sticking one bare ankle out from under the comforter as a way to stay cool. Sleeping in a new place was the worst; motel stays, or sleepovers at a friend's house, or the occasional family camping trip up to northern Minnesota were prescriptions for up-all-night.

To my shock and pleasant surprise, that first night in Ricardo Montalban's mansion (I'd Googled him; he'd been on this early eighties show called *Fantasy Island*), I slept great. In fact, I slept until noon the next day, which normally would be against the law with my parents, but slack was cut in my direction due to the circumstances. I spent the afternoon puttering around, getting to know where everything was in the house, and sitting on the back deck with my MacBook, sending emails to my Mankato friends. I tried to reach Sean a few times, and he tried to reach me, but it was a game of phone tag. No shocker there. Cell reception at the Mankato Mall was always kind of dicey.

So. That night. Hollywood Forever.

Alex drove. Or I should say, Alex's driver drove, since there are restricted licenses in California and you're not supposed to have another kid in the car if you're seventeen. We took her red 1966 BMW convertible, which was awesome and also my first convertible ride ever. The two of us sat in the backseat, drinking Pellegrino water from the bottle, as the driver, a Jamaican man named Sasha, with fabulous dreadlocks to his waist, expertly maneuvered us through the Saturday-night traffic out of the hills, east along Sunset Boulevard, and then onto Santa Monica Boulevard to the cemetery.

I don't mind admitting that the whole death thing scared the crap out of me. Like sometimes I would be hanging out with my friends, or doing homework, or lying in bed at night in that zone between awake and asleep, and suddenly it would hit me that I was going to die. Like, one day there would not be a *me*. At least, not an earthly *me*. I know I'm supposed to take comfort from the whole you-get-to-go-be-with-Jesus thing. But—and please don't tell my mother this—I don't.

Even though Alex had explained the concept of movies at the cemetery, I was having a hard time picturing it. Where I come from, cemeteries are for dead people. And dead people are, well, dead.

As usual, my mother had something to say as I was getting ready to go. She was hanging out with my dad in the kitchen while he baked a sour cream chocolate chip coffee cake.

"Didn't you say that a lot of movie stars are buried there?" she asked me as he spooned the batter into the cake pan.

"Marilyn Monroe. Rudolph Valentino. A bunch of others." I'd done my homework.

"Then I'd say showing movies there makes a lot of sense," my mom concluded. "I hope Marilyn and Rudolph enjoy the show. As for the crowd? I'd say those stars loved crowds."

The cemetery was on the south side of Santa Monica near North Gower, and Sasha dropped us at the entrance, saying that all Alex had to do was text him and he'd be there in fifteen minutes. We got out, and I was happy to see that I'd chosen the right clothing. People were streaming into the cemetery and everyone was dressed down, mostly in T-shirts and jeans, carrying picnic baskets, blankets, and low lawn chairs. I had on Wrangler jeans, an Old Navy white tank top, and a lavender beaded cardigan (from Encore in Old Town, my fave vintage store in Mankato, not that we had more than a few) rolled up in my purse in case it got cool. Alex wore jeans, too, except hers were Denim of Virtue, which I knew from reading the same magazines that every other girl reads cost more than two hundred dollars, and a blue silk hand-embroidered camisole under a sheer white kimono. Her hair was up in an artfully messy bun with tendrils hanging around her face. My hair was in a ponytail. With a scrunchie. When I saw Alex's hair, I quickly pulled the scrunchie out and shoved it into my purse.

We made our donation—ten dollars each—and stepped through the entry gates. The place was huge, all mausoleums, obelisks, and manicured grounds. Alex gave me the quick tour, pointing out the final resting places of Rudolph Valentino, the great director Cecil B. DeMille, and Charlie Chaplin Jr., as we approached the central grassy plaza, where the movie would be projected onto the side of one of the mausoleums. The central plaza itself was covered with people—a few thousand, I'd guess. They were mostly young and mostly beautiful, and the picnics being unpacked were more-than-mostly beautiful, too.

A Mankato picnic would consist of fried chicken, potato salad, coleslaw, and maybe some fruit or homemade cake or cookies, all served up on paper plates. The main beverages would be soft drinks for everyone underage and a beer option for the adults. At Hollywood Forever, as Alex and I snaked around hundreds of picnics in progress, I saw incredible spreads: fruit and cheese plates; Japanese food; Indian food; deli food, like bagels and pastrami; and some of the most mouthwatering barbecue ever. People were eating off china plates with real silverware. The beverages ranged from soft drinks to high-end champagne kept cold in ice-filled buckets.

Guided by text messages, we found Alex's friends. There were four of them, two guys and two girls, on a cherry red blanket with matching gold and red pillows. Alex introduced me around. There was Brooke Summers—alabaster skin and pool blue eyes on a skinny five-foot-five body, with raven black hair in beachy waves to the middle of her back. Brooke wore 7 For All Mankind white jeans that were frayed and ripped up and down each leg. I knew that they came that way, and that these distressed jeans were even more expensive than the ones Alex had on.

There are starving children all over the world. Isn't it kind of just . . . *wrong* to pay *hundreds of dollars* to purchase *new* ripped jeans when you could just buy the *non*-ripped jeans, rip 'em up yourself, and then donate the extra money to charity?

Moving on. The other girl was Skye Lewis. She was nearly six feet tall, with a model-thin body, cheekbones to die for, and short, choppy blond hair. I learned quickly that she was, indeed, a model, who did a lot of catalog work. Suffice it to say, as blessed as she was physically, she was . . . um . . . not too blessed mentally. I would never call her a dumb model, because she was really sweet, plus I hate mean people who say stuff like that, but—full disclosure—I did *think* it for about a nanosecond when she said that elevator buttons confused her, because, like, if she pressed the "up" arrow, did that mean that she *was* up and wanted the elevator to take her *down* or that she was down and wanted the elevator to come take her *up*? I exaggerate only a little.

The first guy I met was Gray Marshall. He was Justin Timberlake cute, with a golden tan, curly dark blond hair, and a muscular body, dressed in black jeans and a fitted plaid button-down. When Alex introduced us, he gave me a convivial hug.

Then there was Brett Goldstein.

I've read stories about girls meeting guys who actually took their breath away. I always figured this stuff only happened in chick flicks starring Kate Hudson. That it happened to me, two nights after I lost my virginity, was a bit much to digest.

Brett was medium tall, with sinewy leg muscles below his cargo shorts, ditto the biceps in his Bob Marley T-shirt. His eyes and hair were the color of Belgian chocolate. He had a defined jawline with a cleft in his chin, shaded by a day or so of stubble, which normally is not a look I go for, because you just know the guy left the stubble so he'd look cool, and trying to look cool is just so . . . not. I'd say he looked like Joe Jonas but I'm not going to—because unlike every other girl who went to my church back in Mankato, I really could not stand the Jonas Brothers' music.

So really, I was prepared not to like Brett. Then he smiled. The grin spread across his face, wide and open. It made his eyes dance.

"Nice to meet you, Natalie." He took my hand, held it,

and looked directly into my eyes, his voice deep and smooth like hot honey and at the same time kind and sincere. "Welcome to L.A.," he added, still holding my hand. "You're going to love it."

Welcome to L.A., Natalie? You're going to love it? Ya think?

An electrical charge shot from his hand into my hand, up my arm, into my head, where it buzzed while my stomach flip-flopped.

"Where'd you move here from?" Brett asked when he finally let go.

"Minnesota," I replied, and added what I hoped was a comical "you betcha" in a Minnesota accent. I figured, when rendered nearly mute by an instant crush, go for the humor. Fortunately, he laughed.

I quickly learned that Skye was his girlfriend. Small detail. But a girl can dream.

We settled down to eat before the movie. They'd brought an astonishing picnic of their own, takeout from a sushi place in Beverly Hills called Yu-N-Mi. It was incredible: sea urchins, mackerel, salmon, ahi, a fantastic roll made from soft-shell crab and shad roe—the only reason I know this is that they told me what each kind of sushi was, since the only kind I'd ever had came packaged at the supermarket in Mankato—and a cooler full of cans of raspberry iced tea and bottled Fiji water.

"What brings you to Los Angeles, Natalie?" Brooke asked after she'd downed a piece of the ahi.

"My mother's a minister," I said. "She was called to a pulpit here."

"At what church?"

"The Church of Beverly Hills. Do you know it?" I asked.

"Know it, don't belong to it," Gray declared. He reached for one of the soft-shell crab rolls. "I'm not really into the whole organized-religion thing."

"Me neither," Skye agreed. "I think Buddhism is pretty cool, though."

Brooke shot her a look. "What do you know about Buddhism?"

Skye pushed her choppy bangs off her forehead. "They don't eat cows, and neither do I."

"We went to In-N-Out Burger yesterday and you polished off a double-double," Brett reminded her.

"That was *hamburger*," Skye pointed out with dignity, licking some wasabi off her pinkie finger. "Not *cow*."

Alex leaned over and kissed Skye on the cheek good-naturedly. "You are one of a kind."

"Maybe not," Skye said. "I also believe in reincarnation."

"Well, I'm Jewish," Brett said, biting into the salmon. "My family goes to Temple Emanuel."

"Like half of Los Angeles," Alex joked. She leaned her head back on Brooke's thigh like they'd been hanging out forever. I learned later they'd been friends since preschool.

"More than that," Brett quipped. "Half a million Jews in Los Angeles, and growing."

Huh. I hadn't thought of that. Back in Mankato, there were a few Jewish families—I knew Caitlin Rosenbloom in my grade, for example. But there wasn't even a synagogue in Mankato. The Jewish kids I knew went to the one in Rochester, seventy-five miles away.

Then Alex, Brooke, Gray, and Skye started playing Do or Die, where you have to choose between having sex with a certain famous person or dying instead—the point being to pick the grossest people possible. Brett didn't join in—which gave him extra points in my book.

"Iced tea?" he asked me as he reached into the cooler.

"Sure." I took the can he offered and popped it open. "Thanks."

"What do you think of Los Angeles so far?" he asked.

I gave a little laugh. "It's . . . big. And I'm living in a big house. I think it belonged to Ricardo Montalban. At least, that's what the real estate agent said."

His eyes rose skyward in surprise. "Damn. Talk about Christian charity," he joked.

I laughed again, uncomfortably. "It's kind of an accident." I told him about the termites at the place on Rodeo Drive.

"Maybe it was all a setup." He popped open his own can of iced tea and gave me a steady look. "To seduce you."

Okay, so I blushed. "Why would anyone want to seduce me?" I blurted out.

The moment these words were out of my mouth, I would have done anything to be playing Do or Die.

He gave me a half smile, clearly aware of how flustered he was making me, and clearly enjoying it. "I meant, to impress your *family*."

"Right," I mumbled. "I knew that."

"Rosie O'Donnell!" Brooke squealed to Gray on the other side of the blanket. "Do or die?"

"I'm already dead," Gray cracked.

57

Brett leaned back, upper body propped up on his elbows. "Tell me about your hometown. Man—*what* is it again?"

"Mankato."

"Fly-over country," Brett said. "That's what they call it here."

I shrugged. "That's kind of small-minded. Anyway, it's their loss. I love it there."

"Tell me about it. Tell me three things that are great."

He said it like he really wanted to know. So I told him. What it was like to walk outside on a June night, strolling through fireflies so thick you thought you were in the middle of the Milky Way. What it was like to wait for the school bus in blinding snow in December, with air so cold the mucus froze in your nose. What it was like to know everyone on your street by their first names, and how if a visitor came from out of state, everyone stopped by to introduce themselves and say hello, with homemade baked goods or a casserole in hand.

"Sounds nice," Brett commented as he reached for a chocolate-covered strawberry in a separate box. "New people moved in next door to us last year. I can't even tell you their name." Instead of eating the strawberry, he held the stem and dangled it near my lips. I opened my mouth and took a bite, feeling both daring and self-conscious. Impossibly beautiful Skye looked over at us and waggled her fingers happily. Evidently she didn't consider me a threat. Well, who could blame her? Not that I would ever *be* a threat, even if Brett was into me. I am not a boy poacher.

I washed the strawberry down with some tea. "I love it there," I told him. "It's home."

"You must miss it already." His voice picked up my sadness.

"I do."

We talked some more, and he told me about some of the really great places in L.A. that I had to visit, like the Santa Monica Pier and the Getty Center. Then it was time for the movie to start.

I have to tell you, there's nothing like watching Tom Hanks and Meg Ryan in the open air on a Los Angeles night. The sound was great and the crowd was into it—three thousand people laughing their heads off and then holding their breath even though they knew that Tom and Meg would meet up. I didn't even mind when I saw Skye rest her head in Brett's lap. Much.

When the movie was over, everyone applauded, then packed up to leave.

"Hey, I've got a great idea," Brooke announced. "Who's up for the lookout at Double P?"

"Pacific Palisades," Skye said, translating for me. "It's on this cliff above the Pacific. You can see all the way down to Long Beach."

Brooke threw her hands in the air and did a sexy little butt wiggle. "Par-tay!" she called.

I looked at Alex. If she wanted to go, it sounded okay to me.

"Forget it," she told Brooke.

"Wuss," Brooke fired back.

"I said forget it, and I mean forget it. I don't go there anymore." Alex was adamant.

"Oh my, it really *is* the new Alex," Brooke jeered.

"Chill," Brett told Brooke under his breath.

"Gawd, since when did everyone get so freaking serious?" Brooke moaned. She pivoted toward Alex. "Why don't you just give up your friends while you're at it?"

Alex's jaw set hard. She took my arm. "Come on, Natalie. We're outta here."

Ten seconds later, we were tramping with the rest of the crowd toward the exit. Brett had said goodbye and that it was good to meet me, but the others were as stony now as they'd been friendly before.

"What was that about?" I asked as Alex texted Sasha to come and pick us up.

"Nothing," she muttered.

Well, that was obviously a lie. But begging a brand-new friend for confidences is stupid. So I leaned against a lamppost as we waited for our ride, doing my best to think about Sean, but with visions of Brett dancing in my head.

Chapter Five

Sunday morning. Church. But not like any church I'd ever been to before.

Call me superstitious or call me eccentric, but I had decided not to set foot in the Church of Beverly Hills until my first worship service. I hadn't engaged in a *total* boycott, though. I'd obviously looked up the church website, seen the pictures, and even taken the virtual tour. I knew that the building could hold two thousand people for a single worship service, that there were a choir of fifty and an orchestra of ten, that there was a Sunday school with an enrollment bigger than some high schools in Minnesota, and that there were two Sunday worship sessions—one from nine until ten-thirty, the second from eleven to twelve-thirty, with a catered luncheon in the church social hall to follow.

My mother, as you can imagine, had help. On the pastoral side, there was a young man—emphasis on "young," since he was still in his mid twenties—named Thomas Bienvenu, who'd graduated from seminary two years before and was the church's junior minister. I hadn't yet met him. Sandra hadn't mentioned him, but the website said he did a lot of work with kids and teens. Thomas and my mom had solid administrative support. There was a well-equipped front office with a full-time administrator, a Sunday school director, and various other staff. It was one of the advantages of a church that didn't have to worry every minute about its budget.

It would have been the easiest thing in the world to stop by and say hello to my mother on Saturday. (In case you don't know, most ministers work six days a week and take Monday off. That is, unless there's a funeral, or a hospital visitation, or a depressed church member who desperately needs to talk, because their life is truly falling apart in front of them. Being a minister is a 24/7/365 gig. Sometimes I don't know how my mom does it. I'm not sure I could. Correction: I know I couldn't.)

Our first Sunday morning in Beverly Hills—the morning after Hollywood Forever—we'd decided that we kids and my dad would go to the second worship service. In fact, my mom had insisted on it, claiming that she'd probably be so nervous at the first one that she'd be mopping her forehead with a handkerchief every other minute. We arrived at the intersection of Santa Monica Boulevard and Palm Drive. The church, a soaring red brick edifice ten stories high, with beautiful stained glass windows that faced the street and a brick multitiered steeple that rose skyward another hundred feet, was located on that corner. At the top of the steeple were carillon bells, which were sounding melodically as we drove up. I recognized the "Ode to Joy" from Beethoven's Ninth Symphony.

"Pretty impressive operation," my dad remarked as he turned the Subaru into the church's underground parking structure, a structure that, according to the church website, could hold eight hundred cars on five levels and had been earthquake-proofed to withstand a temblor of eight on the Richter scale. There were several entrances to and exits from the structure, and uniformed attendants in orange vests were guiding the cars in and out.

Chad raised his eyebrows as he took in the long line of cars waiting to park. "I think we're gonna have to upgrade our vehicle, Dad."

Once again, I saw what he was talking about. BMWs and Mercedes predominated. There were also Audis, Lexuses, and even a few stretch limos. Plus the occasional Bentley, Rolls-Royce, and Ferrari.

My dad shook his head. "Subaru now, Subaru forever."

"I think what Chad is saying is that we don't exactly fit in," Gemma noted, stating the obvious.

"And we're proud of it," Dad declared. "Right, kids?"

Gemma rolled her eyes.

Dad spotted a yellow Lotus pulling out of a spot on the first level, waited for the driver to execute a tight three-point turn, and then pulled us in. "Ready for showtime?"

It turned out he had it right. Sunday-morning worship at the Church of Beverly Hills is, in many ways, showtime.

Start with the congregation itself. As we took the elevator

up to the main level and then made our way through the expansive gold-painted lobby, it felt like we'd stepped into a fashion show. But we weren't sitting in chairs along the runway; we were right in the middle of all the models. I'm not just talking about men and women in their twenties and thirties, either. I'm talking everyone. The kids were gorgeous. The teens were great-looking, with the kinds of hairstyles and clothes you saw in magazines. As for the adults, who ranged from, say, age twenty to moribund, they were thin, well coiffed, tan, and aerobicized within an inch of their lives.

"Oh my God, I'm *fat* compared to these girls!" Gemma hissed. We were walking together, with my father and Chad ahead of us.

"You're not fat," I assured her. But I, too, was taking in the crowd and making unflattering comparisons to myself. "Everyone looks like they stepped out of a movie."

"Botox," Gemma said knowingly. "Nose jobs. Fake boobs. Restylane for pouffy lips." My little sister was frighteningly well informed about this stuff. "We are dressed all wrong!" she moaned. "Why did I listen to you?"

Gemma and I had consulted in the morning and decided that the things to wear to our first day of church were our new dresses from Target. Mine was green and sleeveless and came to just above my knees. Gemma's was the same length but a pink and orange paisley babydoll style. Both dresses had modest necklines. As for my dad and brother, they looked like father and son in sport coat/white shirt/tie/khaki trouser combinations.

I took in the clothes other girls our age were wearing.

Their dresses and skirts were inches shorter than ours, not to mention infinitely more expensive. Everywhere you looked, it seemed like the ultra-pricey boutiques of Rodeo Drive had migrated a few blocks east and emptied their stock onto this congregation.

"You look great," I told Gemma.

"I look like I'm from Minne-freaking-sota," Gemma shot back.

We entered the main sanctuary, which was already three-quarters filled. In Mankato, our church was a model of simplicity: fifteen double rows of pews that stretched from the slightly raised stage at the front, where my mother would deliver her sermons, and a couple of inspirational tapestries on the wall. There was a single cross at the front of the space and crosses carved into the sides of each pew. Large windows let in natural light. That was it.

Like I said, I'd taken the virtual tour, but it didn't prepare me for the vastness of the Church of Beverly Hills. More than anything, the church reminded me of theater in the round, with a semicircle of seats around a central raised area, and another stage at the west end of the sanctuary. There was a raised section for the choir—already seated, in fitted jackets and trousers instead of the usual choir robes—and a sunken orchestra pit. From the outside of the building, the stained glass was pretty. From the inside, the ten windows, each depicting an abstract vision of one of the Ten Commandments, were positively breathtaking as the morning sun poured through, dancing colors across the comfortable individual seats, each of which had a rack for a Bible and a hymnal. The one thing I wasn't impressed with was that there was no welcome table for visitors. We had that in Minnesota. Even though on a typical Sunday in Mankato, the welcome table was kind of pointless. Everyone knew everyone else. Here, how would you tell who was new and who wasn't?

"Hey!" Gemma exclaimed. "There's Lisa!" She waved, and I spotted the girl from the youth group who'd taken Gemma through our new house. She was sitting with four or five other kids and motioning to Gemma to come and join them. Without a word to me, Gemma took off in their direction.

"Find us at lunch, okay?" I called to her.

She nodded to me over her shoulder. I saw Lisa hug Gemma, then excitedly introduce her to the others, who hugged Gemma, too. That was nice.

That's when I heard my name being called in a loud whisper. "Natalie!"

I turned around. There was Sandra, motioning to me to sit with her and some other kids. Any other time, I would have— my parents always said that you can see your family all the time, but sometimes you only saw your friends in church, so why not sit with them? But not on this first day. Not if Gemma was with Lisa. So I mouthed, "At lunch," to Sandra, pointed to where my dad and Chad were sitting, and shrugged. She gave an understanding smile and a little wave.

My seat was next to my dad, with Chad on his other side. My father leaned toward me discreetly. "I saw what you did with Gemma. Smart."

"Thanks." I breathed a little easier, though not so easy that I could help getting an extra strong whiff of the Chanel

No 5 perfume the woman to my left was wearing. Two years earlier, Gemma, Chad, and I had saved up and pooled our allowances to buy my mom the smallest bottle possible for Mother's Day. She saved it for special occasions.

My brother leaned across my dad toward me. "Did you see who's here?" He was truly excited.

"Um . . . a lot of Christian people?"

My dad laughed.

"Kelly Clarkson. About five rows ahead, and to the left."

As I looked for her, I had a celebrity spotting of my own. Kristen Kreuk, chatting amiably with an older gentleman in a white linen suit.

Okay. This really was the church of the rich and famous. And us.

A moment later, worship started. To my relief, it followed basically the same form as back home. It opened with singing and praise. In Mankato, this was usually a song or two. Here it was a full fifteen minutes, with instrumentals from the orchestra, chorale singing, and one absolutely stunning solo by a middle-aged woman. The woman next to me whispered that she was one of the most sought-after commercial-jingle singers in town. The words to every song were projected on two large telescreens that lowered from the ceiling, so everyone could follow along. And follow along they did. The atmosphere was fun, even a little bit raucous. And this was before my mother came out to lead the service.

Then the music stopped, and my mom appeared from behind the GOD IS LOVE curtain at the front of the sanctuary. Shockingly, she was wearing the same worship robe she used to wear in Minnesota. Black, with a quirky red stripe that started at the neckline, passed over her heart, and ran down to the base of the gown. I asked her once whether the red stripe had religious significance. No, she said with a conspiratorial grin. She just liked how it looked. No obvious crucifix, though I knew she wore a small silver one habitually.

To my surprise, the congregation rose as one to applaud her. Really loudly. So loudly that it felt like the bricks of the building might shake loose.

We stood and clapped, too, my father loudest of all. His face beamed with pride as he raised his hands over his head so my mom could see him. She did, and gave the little secret smile that she thought only they knew, but that I recognized. She was so loved by him. Did Sean love me that way? He said he loved me. But what did that mean? Did it mean that the next time I saw him, whenever that would be, he'd expect me—

I willed my brain to stop thinking about Sean and sex. Which meant my brain immediately went to thoughts of Brett Goldstein and sex. In church. God help me. I mean it.

My mother thanked her congregation for the warm welcome. To my surprise, she introduced Chad, Gemma, and me by name, but spared us the embarrassment of making us stand, saying everyone would get to know us well enough in the days to come. "Maybe too well," she added, to warm laughter. Then she introduced Dad, calling him the love of her life and thanking him for deciding with her to accept this pulpit.

Finally, she opened her Bible. "Today's lesson is from the Epistle of James. Follow with me, please. And you'll also want to flip to Leviticus, Chapter Nineteen. I'll give you the verse when we get to it."

Chad and I looked at each other. We've heard our mom preach—a lot. Never on James, though. We opened our New Testaments to James, and my mother spoke beautifully and movingly about the relationship between James and his brother Jesus, and about James's injunction to treat rich and poor the same way, with the same open heart. She linked it to the section of Leviticus about not favoring a person because they are rich or poor.

"Ladies and gentlemen of my new home," my mother said, "judge me not by where I stand, because this stage is not me. Judge me not by the robe I wear. I am not my robe. Judge me not by my title, or the number of books on the shelves in my office—and the movers will tell you that I nearly ruined their backs. Judge me as Jesus himself would judge me. Judge me as you would want Jesus to judge you."

The congregation was both absolutely rapt and a little embarrassed. I saw a few people unconsciously touching their expensive pocketbooks and designer clothes, or scuffing their designer shoes on the parquet floor. This was vintage Marsha Shelton. The church leadership had to have known the kind of woman they were hiring. They chose my mom.

The service ended a half hour later, after some of the best church singing I'd ever heard and a welcome from Kent Stevens, one of the leading board members. Stevens invited the congregation to come to the church social hall afterward for a buffet.

"We brought in the catering trucks from James Cameron's *Avatar*. I suspect about half of you worked on that picture," he quipped. "And if you're working for Jim, you know there'll be another movie from him for you to work on . . . in about eight years!" The congregation roared with laughter at the inside joke, and I learned later that Cameron takes a really, really long time to prep his films. Then the orchestra struck up an inspiring closing instrumental, and the service was over.

Lunch. In Mankato, it was pimento-and-cheese sandwiches with the crusts cut off, made by the lunch committee. Here? Well, it was a little different.

At least five hundred people stayed. The food was served outside under a huge multicolored tent. You got your food there and brought it inside to one of the scores of long tables that had been set with cutlery. Uniformed servers circulated with pitchers of iced tea and juice. The menu included roasted fresh salmon and albacore, vegetables from the farmers' market, dark bread baked in the kitchen, and zucchini lasagna for the vegetarians in the crowd. I noticed the lasagna going very fast.

As I joined the buffet line, I saw Gemma and Lisa ahead of me, with Chad. Something Chad was saying had to be funny, because Lisa was laughing uproariously. Gemma caught my eye and gave a happy wave. I waved back, glad that my mother hadn't made us stand when she'd introduced us. I was feeling conspicuous enough in my Target dress, even with my mother's sermon fresh in my ears.

"Hey, Natalie!" Sandra came up to me with a few people our age in tow. "I want you to meet my friends. This is Natalie Shelton," she announced. "Wasn't her mom amazing?"

I heard a chorus of "definitely," "for sure," "you're so lucky to have her as a mom." Plus a barrage of names that I couldn't hope to remember. Suddenly, I was a celebrity. One person was offering to bring me a plate of food. Another one, dessert. Another, something from the fruit boat. Sandra directed traffic, telling everyone that she would walk me to a table and save seats. At least I remembered to say thank you.

"What do you think?" she asked as we wended our way back into the social hall.

"Impressive," I said honestly.

"I know! And you're going to love them. So much better than Alex Samuels. *Serious* bad news." She actually shuddered.

There it was. Not five minutes into the convo, and Alex's name came up like she was the Antichrist. Well. I could choose my own friends, thank you very much.

"We hung out last night. It was fun." I said it like I didn't have a care in the world.

Sandra scowled as she led me to my table. "You need to listen to your mother's sermon a little better. Alex is snowing you."

"No she isn't."

"Yes she is." Sandra pulled a chair out for me. "I'm about to give you some excellent advice. Google her. That's all I'm saying." She slid into the seat next to mine.

Before I could get any more information, Sandra's friends came back with our food, and the talk was about everything but what I wanted to talk about: my new friend Alex Samuels.

Chapter Six

We didn't get back to Ricardo's mansion—I definitely did not think of it as "home"—until nearly five-thirty. The luncheon had stretched into midafternoon, then late afternoon. Typically, the minister and his or her family are the last to leave these kinds of affairs. Back in Minnesota, on a typical Sunday, it didn't matter much. Folks wanted to get home to watch the Vikings or the Packers, or go fishing or ice fishing, or work in their gardens (depending on the season), and the food at church wasn't all that great to begin with.

Well, this wasn't Minnesota, and this wasn't a typical Sunday. Los Angeles didn't have a football team even during football season, fishing wasn't popular, and it seemed as if everyone employed Mexican gardeners instead of tilling the soil themselves. More than that, this first Sunday luncheon at church was a bit of a freak show, and my family was the main attraction. Most people kept a polite distance at the beginning, though I could feel the eyes on me. As the meal went on, polite distance gave way to "Hi, I just wanted to meet you." From *everyone*. Young, old, and in between. For someone who isn't good with names—namely, me—this can be a challenge. Besides, unlike my sister, I don't like being stared at. Maybe if I looked like Gemma instead of looking like me, I'd feel differently.

Lisa Stevens had come back to the house with us. She, Gemma, and Chad were getting into the hot tub. They invited me, but I pled exhaustion and went up to my room.

I was about to do something I never do. Google someone. Namely, Alex.

Okay. I realize a lot of people Google every single person they meet and don't think anything of it. Not me. It just feels . . . wrong. I've never even Googled myself.

But I couldn't get Sandra's words out of my head. They drove me crazy throughout lunch. I had to do it. For my own sanity.

I left a message for Sean to call me—we still hadn't talked—changed out of my church dress into a pair of shorts and a faded blue T-shirt, and sat down at my MacBook to open Safari when my cell sounded with Sean's distinct ringtone. Finally!

"Hey, you!" I was glad to hear from him. We had a lot to talk about, if he was willing.

"Hey, you, yourself." He chuckled. "That California life must be agreeing with you. You're a hard girl to reach."

"You're not so easy yourself," I fired back.

"I've been pretty busy." He launched into a detailed litany

of what had gone on in Mankato in the two days I'd been away. He'd gone to my old church that morning, and reported on his experience.

"The new pastor who replaced your mom? Well, he's not even half as good as your mom."

"I'll tell her that." I smiled.

"I bet everyone loves her. What was her first day like?"

I leaned forward to stretch my back. We were talking like we always did, about this and that. Easily. Companionably. But we weren't talking about the biggest thing of all.

"There's a lot to tell. I'll send you an email." I hesitated. Then I leaped. "Sean?"

"Yeah?"

"Why aren't we talking about it?"

Silence. Then, finally . . .

"What's to talk about?" Sean asked. "It happened. It probably shouldn't have happened, but it happened. Talking about it won't change it."

I pressed. "I know that. But how do you *feel?*"

His answer was immediate. "I just told you how I feel."

"No you didn't. You told me what you thought. You didn't say how you feel."

He was quiet again for a moment. "Well, why don't you start, if you want to talk about how we feel?"

"Okay. I will."

Mind you, I had no idea what I was going to say. But I found myself pouring out my heart and soul to Sean, and it was all about my feelings.

"I'm ashamed of myself, for doing something that I never thought I would do until I was married, and that I didn't

74

want to do until I was married. I'm guilty, so guilty that I don't want to talk about it with anyone but you. I'm ashamed that I'm hiding it from my parents and especially my mom, because I don't want her to think badly of me." I was rolling now. "I'm disappointed, because honestly it wasn't such a great experience, and I didn't enjoy it all that much."

"No?"

"No," I said, "I didn't. I didn't love it. And now I'm worried that it's what it's going to be like for the rest of my life. That I somehow polluted myself, and polluted us, and polluted all my hopes and dreams. But part of me is glad, too. I mean, I feel like I'm not a kid anymore."

Silence again.

"Sean? That's how I feel. Actually, that's the start of how I feel. Just the beginning of how I feel. Now, I'd like to know how you feel, too."

As I urged Sean to talk, a hummingbird flew up and suspended at a feeder right outside my window that I hadn't even noticed, his long beak dipping into the sweet red nectar, his wings flapping furiously. He was working so hard, I thought, to stay in the same place. Then, like a flash of ruby-throated light, he was gone.

"It's hard on the phone," Sean said.

"I know. It was hard for me, too. But I just did it." It seemed like he was dodging.

"How about if we talk face to face? I can come to Los Angeles in a few weeks."

What?

That is exactly what I thought. What I said was "Really?"

"My sister has frequent-flier miles," Sean explained, "and

she's flying to New York for some business thing at the end of the month. She'll get more miles for that, and she said she'll give me a ticket. Isn't that great?"

Sean's sister was ten years older than him and worked for Bank of America. She was constantly flying here and there from her base in Minneapolis.

"That's . . . that's amazing."

What else could I have said? Don't come? I want to force you to talk to me about your feelings before you come? That would have broken his heart.

"Then I'll keep you posted on my plans so you can check it with your parents." His voice was lighter now that he was back on unemotional territory. Then his sister beeped in, and he had to go, and we said goodbye.

Honestly? I didn't mind. It had been a frustrating conversation. I'd put myself out there for him, and he hadn't reciprocated. It left me feeling empty.

A few moments later, my Mac had booted up, and Alex's name stared at me from inside quotation marks on Google's main page. All I had to do was push "Google Search."

I didn't have to do it. But I did. It took 0.14 seconds for 134,000 Google hits to pop up. The lead links were taken from Google News. I didn't even have to read the articles. I got all the information I needed from the links themselves.

ALEX SHELTON DRUGGING IN REHAB RUMORS
DENIED—14 *days ago*
Teen party girl *Alex Shelton* has been forced
to deny claims that she has smuggled drugs

and alcohol into an Arizona rehabilitation facility where she has been ensconced for the last month. Another rehab patient made the allegations . . .
all 79 news articles »

LAUREN CONRAD WEIGHS IN ON THE ALEX SHELTON NAKED ON HOLLYWOOD BOULEVARD INCIDENT—MTV.com
all 626 news articles »

ALEX SHELTON CROWNED PARTY GIRL OF THE YEAR BY *LA WEEKLY*, WINNING THE UNDER-17 DIVISION. "There really was no competition," says the editor of the alternative weekly. Shelton, the sister of sex, drugs, and rock 'n' roll guitar player Shepard Shelton, and daughter of deceased record . . .
all 84 news articles »

There were a dozen links like this. Under those were the "Image Results," just in case anyone might have thought that the Alex Samuels of the articles was a different Alex Samuels, in a different Beverly Hills, in an alternative universe.

Alex on the beach, posing in the bottom half of a string bikini.

Alex on the red carpet at the Teen Choice Awards with Vanessa Hudgens.

Alex in a crowded nightclub, toasting the camera with a

martini glass in one hand and a raised middle finger on the other.

Alex outside House of Blues, sprawled on the ground, puking in the gutter.

That was it. I couldn't take any more. I slammed my finger down on my laptop power button and turned it off.

A moment later, though, I was booting up my Mac again. Going to Google again. Then reading dozens, scores, maybe hundreds of newspaper articles and blog entries about my new maybe-friend Alex.

Alex Samuels was notorious. A club kid since the age of thirteen, she'd done every drug in the book and then some. She'd been arrested for shoplifting and public indecency, been kicked out of two private schools and one public school, thought nothing of dropping tens of thousands of dollars on clothes, meals, and jewelry, and—this was maybe worst of all—been accused of giving Ecstasy and LSD to some junior high students at her last school. She had spent the entire month of May and part of June of that year in rehab in Arizona, at an exclusive center that cost a thousand dollars a day. That was, however, not her first experience with rehab. She'd tried twice before. Each time, it had taken less than a month for her to return to her partying ways.

This time when I shut down my laptop, it was for good. I went to the window, which had a little seat by it, and stared into the distance, past the hummingbird feeder, and across the arroyo between our place and Alex's. As I sat there, the hummingbird returned, but the whirring of his wings barely registered.

Look, I may be the eldest daughter of a minister, but I am not, and was not, naïve. Mankato, Minnesota, may not be Los Angeles or New York, but it's not, like, Mars. We have drinking, we have drugs, we have girls who get pregnant in ninth grade, we have guys who are strung out on crystal meth and everyone knows it. Kids go to juvie, kids get polluted and wreck their cars. Last year, a guy in my math class drank so much that he barfed and inhaled his own vomit. I think he's still in the hospital.

I hope my non-hayseed credentials are now hereby established. That said, in comparison to anything or anyone I'd encountered in my former life, Alex scared me. Yet the Alex Samuels of the past was not the Alex I'd met. Still, she'd tried rehab before. Failed before. *Twice.*

What to do?

Eat. Ice cream. Now.

I went downstairs to the kitchen, where I knew my dad had laid in a hefty supply of Baskin-Robbins rocky road, his favorite. I preferred mint chip, but I didn't much care about the flavor in my current mental state; rocky road would have to do.

Maybe my folks were in a mental state, too. They'd each changed into a variation of the clothes I was wearing; I found them sitting side by side at the kitchen bar, digging into the rocky road container with two spoons.

My mom smiled wearily at me. "Hi, sweetie."

Her voice was tired. No shocker there. She must be completely exhausted.

"Grab a spoon," my dad suggested.

I did, then sat next to Mom and put said spoon to work.

"What's going on, Nat?" My mother's voice was gentle.

Let me say this about parents right now. While it is not a fashionable thing to talk to one's parents, and while it doesn't happen very often on television shows on the CW or in teen novels about rich girls in New York City or here in Los Angeles or at private school, and while advice columns are full of tips for parents on how to talk to their teens, I would guess that a lot more kids my age actually *do* converse with their mom and/or dad and respect their opinions than don't.

You don't have to remind me that I wasn't willing to talk to my parents about Sean.

I'm a long, long, long way from perfect.

We did talk about Alex, though. I told them that we'd spent an afternoon and an evening together, that I really liked her, that she'd been nothing but decent to me. I told them how ashamed I was that I'd Googled her, and then how upset I was about what I'd learned.

My folks looked at each other when I was done.

"What?" I asked. "What do you think?"

"I don't know," my mother replied.

Huh. She almost never said "I don't know."

"I think what your mom is saying is she and I want some time to talk about all this." My father gave his ice cream spoon a final lick.

"I'm worried about you," my mother admitted.

My father turned to her, his jaw set. "I'm not worried about Nat. I'm worried about this girl."

"I'm worried about her *and* this girl." My mom's gaze

shifted to me. "The Googling? I could go either way. As for what you learned, you would have found out eventually. And I'm guessing the reason you Googled her is that someone else told you something about Alex."

"I didn't want to believe that it was true," I admitted.

"Then you did hear something. It's human nature. Bad news travels fast." She put the lid on the ice cream. "Gossip travels faster."

"Her parents are dead, Mom," I said, rising to stick my spoon in the dishwasher. "In a plane crash. If anything happened to you guys? I might turn to drugs, too."

"Poor kid," my dad murmured. "Your mom and I need to talk about this, Nat."

"It can wait till tomorrow." I hoped I was being helpful. I also hoped I wasn't going to have to face some kind of ultimatum from my parents about Alex. They'd never forbidden me to have a friend before, but we'd never lived in Beverly Hills before, either, and I'd never had a friend like Alex Samuels.

"I don't think we want to wait. Do we, Marsha?" My dad raised his eyebrows at my mom, who shook her head.

"No. I want to think about this now. And talk about this now," my mom agreed. "Nat, how about we check in with you in an hour?"

I nodded. I had some thinking to do, too. Maybe this was the kind of friendship I wanted to pursue. On the other hand, maybe it wasn't.

Chapter Seven

While I waited for my parents to call or text me—Ricardo's mansion was so big that cell phones had become the main means of getting someone's attention—to come back downstairs to talk to them, I opened my lyric notebook and took a look at what I had on paper for "The Shape I'm In."

The sun sets bright, it rises dim,
That's the measure of the shape I'm in.
The ice it warms me, the heat it chills,
That's the measure of the games and the thrills.
The sun sets bright, it rises dim,
That's the measure of the shape I'm in.

Sleep wears me out, life makes me sleep,
That's the measure when I try to go deep.
The sun sets bright, it rises dim,
That's the measure of the shape I'm in.

It wasn't bad. It wasn't great. It needed a lot of work. The thing was, I'd started a week before we moved, in anticipation of how I might feel after the move. Now that we'd actually moved, the lyrics seemed, well, inadequate. I tried for the next forty-five minutes to improve them, until the knock came at my door.

"Nat? Can we come in?" My father's voice was calm but had that undertone that brooked no opposition. In other words, they were coming in whether I said okay or not. Yes, that *is* annoying.

"Okay."

The hour break had actually turned out to be a good idea. It gave me time to think between futile stabs at my lyrics. Thinking for me never involved just sitting in a chair and staring into the night. I'm one of those people who do their best thinking while doing something else. Cleaning out the closet. Taking a shower. Or most often, playing music or writing songs.

"Hey," my mother said. She'd changed into her favorite gingham bathrobe, given to her as a Christmas gift by one of our parishioners in Minnesota.

"Hi." I leaned my guitar against my bed.

My folks sat on the floor with me. "We've been talking."

"And I've been thinking," I replied honestly. Not that my thinking had gotten me anywhere. The whole sex-drugs-Hollywood thing was so not me. But apparently, it was very much Alex and her friends.

"What your father and I think matters," my mom declared. "But it doesn't matter as much as what you think, Nat. So?"

"I don't know what to do," I admitted, staring at the woven rug.

My mom cocked her head at me. "Have you prayed about it?"

"Honestly? No." That was the truth. "I wanted to think rationally about this one."

A small smile tweaked the edges of my mom's mouth. "They're not mutually exclusive, you know."

"Sometimes prayer helps you be still enough to listen to your own inner voice," my dad added.

Like I hadn't heard *that* one from him a thousand times. "I know."

"At the risk of stating the obvious, I can't tell you I'm thrilled with the choices Alex has made," my mom said. "But evidently she's trying to change. We have enough confidence that you'll be true to your own values, no matter what."

Dad stood and went to the window. "What's your biggest fear?" he asked as he looked toward the hills.

"That Alex has a lot of problems that I can't handle. That I'll be her friend, and then she'll do something that scares me." I stretched my legs out and bent to touch my fingertips to my toes. Normally, it would be no problem for me to do that. It was now, after the call with Sean and what I'd learned about Alex. I was tense. I got even more tense as I thought of Sandra and the church kids I'd met.

"There's more," I said. "The girls from church? They won't like me for liking Alex. Sandra warned me to stay away from her." I thought about that for a moment. "Which kind of ticks me off."

Dad turned away from the window. "She probably thought she was doing you a favor."

I folded my arms. "Well, she wasn't."

My mom nudged me with her foot. "Who knows? Maybe Alex will come to church with you some Sunday, and you'll help Sandra and Alex become friends."

Right. And maybe I'll grow a third breast. But I doubt it.

"It's possible," my dad chimed in. "You won't know unless you try."

The level of naïveté in my bedroom at that moment was breathtaking. It was the kind of parentally blind statement that would make anyone—including me—question the validity of anything else that came out of their lips. It was more likely that I could get Modest Mouse to ask Miley to be their new lead singer than broker a friendship between Sandra and Alex.

Fortunately, my folks picked that moment to say good night.

Great. How helpful. Not that there was anything they could have said or done differently. In a sense, they were absolutely right. It really was my decision.

I sat on my bed and fished my cell phone out of my pocket. I had put Alex's number on speed dial. She picked up on the second ring.

"Hey, Nat." She sounded happy to hear from me. "How are you?"

"Not so good," I told her. My heart started to pound. "We need to talk."

When I reached her, she was in Beverly Hills, getting her eyebrows done and eyelash extensions put in at Valerie's, which I later learned was one of the top salons on Rodeo Drive. She'd invited me to come by—Valerie had opened the place for her—and assured me that the queen of Beverly Hills beauty would be happy to work her magic on me. What girl couldn't use a little of Valerie's magic? I demurred—not that I was morally opposed!—and wondered aloud if there was someplace we could meet afterward. She suggested the Ivy, on Robertson Boulevard. It was a beautiful evening, they had a great terrace, and I'd definitely be able to do some celebrity sighting. Cell phone photos for my friends in Minnesota, however, were discouraged.

"A lot of the really big stars have bodyguards," Alex explained. "Some tourist will snap a photo and the bodyguard will follow the poor schmuck to their car and demand their phone. Then he'll crush it like a cockroach. It can get ugly."

I put on a clean pair of jeans and a black tank top, brushed my hair, and applied some mascara and lip gloss. Then I explained to my parents that I was going to meet Alex, MapQuested directions, and drove the Saturn to the west side of Robertson between Beverly and West Third. The Ivy valets gave me the most bemused look ever when I handed over the keys. Evidently, Saturns were the moral equivalent of rickshaws. Yet I took the valet ticket and gave my name to the petite Asian hostess inside the white picket fence atop the low brick wall that separated the patio from the street, just like Alex had instructed.

"Ms. Shelton? Alex isn't here yet. But we've got a wonderful table for you. Follow me."

I did. The patio was filled with beautiful people chattering and eating at circular tables under big white umbrellas. The night was warm and still; I felt like I was walking onto a movie set. Then I realized I very well could have seen a movie scene that had been set right here. So the slight sense of déjà vu was not unwarranted.

"Natalie Shelton?"

Someone behind me called my name. But it couldn't be Alex. She wasn't here.

I turned. A handsome couple in their early forties—the guy in a white button-down shirt and jeans, the woman with thick lush blond hair and an enviable figure—beckoned to me. They looked vaguely, *very* vaguely, familiar.

"Hi!" The man greeted me warmly. "We're Ben and Cecilia."

"Do I know you?" I asked.

"We met you at lunch today," Cecilia said with a smile. "We're members of the church."

I must have looked embarrassed, because Ben came to my rescue. "Hey, no biggie if you don't remember. I bet you met five hundred people today. Anyway, we just wanted to say hello. Are you here with friends? Do you want to join us?"

"I'm—I'm meeting someone," I told them.

"Then enjoy. The artichoke pizza is to die for," Cecilia confided. "We'll see you around. Welcome to L.A."

I shook hands with them, thinking that maybe this was something not so different from Mankato. That is, there wasn't a single place I could go in Mankato without someone knowing me as the minister's daughter. The supermarket, the hardware store, the bowling alley, the roller rink, the library—it didn't matter. Even though our church was small, everyone knew who I was. As my mom's radio show got bigger, it got worse. I felt like I was constantly watched. Constantly evaluated. Constantly judged. Now here I was, two thousand miles away, and it was exactly the same thing. Only with more expensive clothes, better perfume, and longer menus.

I turned back toward my table and found Alex arriving to meet me. In fact, she'd caught the whole scene with Ben and Cecilia.

"You're a celebrity," she joked as she scooted over to the left so that I could sit easily. "In town for three days, already met Ben and Cecilia Burdette."

"Are they someone I should know?"

Alex tilted her head back and laughed. "Only if you want to be an actor or a writer. He's, like, the biggest entertainment lawyer in town."

"I'll keep that in mind."

A waitress—one with wild red hair, chiseled cheekbones, and ruby lips—suddenly materialized at our table. "Alex? Ready to eat?"

Alex smiled at her. "I'm starving."

"No menus?" I asked.

"No need. Trust me, I know what's good here," Alex replied.

I watched as the waitress efficiently poured two glasses of iced tea, put a wicker basket of home-baked breads at one side of the table, and placed a small artichoke-covered pizza atop a wire platter holder. It smelled heavenly.

"Enjoy, you two." The waitress moved off. The moment she did, Alex faced me.

Okay. Her eyebrows were gorgeous, with nary a stray hair. Her eyelashes had gotten five times thicker and twice as long, not that they'd needed a lot of cosmetic support to begin with.

"You wanted to talk. What's going on?" she asked.

My heart pounded. There was no easy way to admit this.

"Someone at my church talked about you. She said I should Google you, and . . . I did." I said it quickly, like ripping a bandage off an open wound.

Alex looked at me quizzically. Then she laughed heartily. "That's it? Someone told you to Google me, and you did?"

"I feel terrible!"

The laughter kept coming. It was okay at first. Then I felt offended. Maybe it was funny to her. It wasn't funny to me.

"Look," I said quietly. "I think Googling a friend sucks."

"Please," Alex scoffed, reaching for a slice of pizza. She licked some tomato sauce off her pinkie. "Out here it's a com-pliment. People compete to see who has the most hits. You really have to try the pizza."

I put a slice on my plate. "What I did still sucks."

Alex bit into her pizza and washed it down with some iced tea. "You don't feel bad about what you did, you feel bad about what you found out," she clarified. "Believe me, if you'd found out I'd won an MTV Movie Award as best new actress, you wouldn't feel bad. You'd be complimenting me for my incredible modesty. Instead, you read a bunch of horror stories and now you're wondering, who is this chick? Right?" She smiled again, as if to defuse the intensity of what she'd just said.

I tasted the tea, which had hints of rose and lilac. Delicious.

"That's part of it," I allowed. "But I do feel bad about the Googling. It's like, I don't know, an invasion of your privacy."

"If it's on Google, Natalie? It's not private."

I nodded. She had a point.

"Besides," she went on, "this is Hollywood. Everyone Googles everyone else. And ZabaSearch, and 123people. I know kids who have a yearly subscription to Intelius. I think they know more about me than I know about myself. I Googled you. Not much out there. Lots of church-mission pictures. And someone on Facebook who doesn't like you."

"Who?"

Alex waggled her newly perfected eyebrows. "Check yourself out online. You might learn something." She cocked her head toward the slice of pizza on my plate. "You're supposed to taste it."

We ate in silence for a while. I saw Leonardo DiCaprio, baseball cap down low, come onto the patio to eat. Lil' Kim sashayed inside with an entourage. Other than that, I concentrated on my food. It was a good excuse for not talking, seeing as how I still wasn't sure what more I wanted to say.

Alex called me on it.

"You didn't ask me to meet you to talk about the guilt of Googling," she pointed out as she finished her third small slice. "So you want to discuss my past, or not?"

"How much is true?"

She countered with a question of her own. "What's the worst thing you've ever done? I mean it. The worst. Don't hold back."

Yeah. The sex-with-Sean thing, in my opinion, but maybe not in Alex's. I racked my brain for something else.

"Some friends and I got caught skinny-dipping in the pond at the Mankato Country Club. By the police."

"Guys and girls?" Alex asked.

I shook my head. "Just girls."

"You wild woman," Alex teased.

"It was Christmas Eve," I added, trying to up my cool quotient. It was true. We'd had a warm spell in Mankato, and temps were in the sixties, which is pretty warm for Minnesota. Some friends and I decided to go skinny-dipping. "It was a quick dip."

She sipped more tea. "And then there's me. I've stolen, driven drunk, and lost my license. I've driven drunk *without* a license. I've done E, LSD, smack, and crack. I lost my virginity when I was fourteen to a guy I didn't know. I've embarrassed myself in public more times than I can count. And here's the topper: I thought it was cool."

"Were you planning to tell me all this?" I asked, nervously refolding my napkin.

"Eventually. I mean, I don't think I need to wear it on a sign around my neck. Like *Welcome to Beverly Hills, and by the way, I am a bad, bad girl.*"

Was that a tear I saw in the corner of her left eye? It was gone as quickly as it had appeared.

I took in the gorgeous people on the deck. A lot of laughter and a lot of preening. None of them seemed to be in a conversation as serious as ours.

Then I felt Alex's hand on my arm and turned back to her.

"You know I'm out of rehab now," she stated.

"Yeah. And I think it's great."

"It is great. I really think I have a chance this time. Somehow, it's different." She spotted someone she knew across the patio and gave a little wave of acknowledgement. "I'm living honestly, one day at a time."

"Then I'm going to be honest, too," I told her. "I'm worried about being your friend. We're really different. I'm not a party girl. I never was, and I never will be."

She stared into my eyes. "It's not who I want to be anymore."

I felt guilty even bringing this up, but I thought it was important. "You did rehab before."

"And it didn't take. I guess you got that one off the Internet. If at first you don't succeed . . ." She balled her napkin up and tossed it onto her plate. "Look, that was then, and this is now. It wasn't hard to figure out that you're not a party girl. I mean, you might even be the oldest living virgin in Beverly Hills."

Um . . . not exactly. I smiled weakly.

"I believe people can change," Alex continued. "*I* can change. Do you believe me?"

I nodded.

"I'm a girl with a million scars. But I'm up front about all of them." She raked her hair off her face. "The only people I truly cannot stand are the hypocrites. The ones who pretend to be someone they're not."

I flushed. Right at that moment, I felt like the biggest hypocrite in the world.

"I want you to be my friend. But if you are? I've done what

I've done. I'm not proud of it. And I'm not playing poor-little-rich-girl-whose-parents-died, either. It's my life; I'm taking responsibility for it." She grinned. "Who knows? Maybe you'll be a good influence on me."

In that moment, I finally made up my mind. I wanted to be her friend.

I smiled at her. "Maybe I will."

Chapter Eight

My grandmother—my father's mother—Palma Shelton owns a farm in northern Iowa near a town called Manly, and I am not making that up. She has forty acres; my uncle Clarence Shelton and his wife, Lila, live just down the road with their children and tend another forty acres. Since Palma isn't young anymore, Clarence and Lila help her with the land. They grow corn, soybeans, wheat, and alfalfa. They also have animals, like cows, goats, and chickens. About two hundred chickens, to be precise, that produce an awful lot of eggs. The chickens live in a chicken shack on Clarence and Lila's property.

There's a point to all this.

On Tuesday night, our family was invited to the home of Kent Stevens (father of Lisa Stevens, Gemma's new BFF) for a barbecue. Kent Stevens's mansion made Ricardo's mansion look like Clarence and Lila's chicken shack.

Before we went over there, I did a Google search of Kent.

That's one thing about doing something that's kind of wrong. The first time you do it, you can have all kinds of moral qualms. The second time, it's a lot easier. By the third time, it takes on a kind of normalcy and you don't even blink. Which is why it's better not to do it the first time. Not that I was thinking in that direction when Sean and I got down on the cabin floor, but still.

Anyway, I honestly had never heard of Kent before we arrived in Los Angeles. There are Hollywood moguls who do their best to stay in the public eye. Then there are those no one has heard of, who are often richer and more powerful than the people you have heard of.

Kent Stevens fits into the latter category. There were very few articles about him, except for those that either called him a "private person" or gushed about his seven-figure donations to this charity or that charity, including our church. Kent and his wife, Joan, were on the boards of the opera, the Mark Taper Forum, and the Los Angeles Museum of Contemporary Art. According to what I read, they specialized in raising money from their über-rich friends for various causes and then topping all the other donations with their own.

Kent was the executive producer of four network episodic television shows, had a movie production company with guaranteed financing from Columbia TriStar for several twenty- to fifty-million-dollar pictures a year, and also produced television and movie-theater commercials. I was shocked by how lucrative that was, how much a drug company, like Pfizer, pays to get you to buy their brand of heartburn squelcher or cholesterol blocker.

Oh yeah. For fun? He owned the largest exotic-car

dealership in the western United States, located on the Miracle Mile near CBS's production studios. Half the Lotuses, Ferraris, Porsches, Bentleys, Jaguars, and Alfa Romeos—especially the classic ones from thirty and forty years ago—on the road came through his dealership.

Ka-ching.

We drove to his house in the Subaru. Or I should say, we drove to the gate of his house in the Subaru. No mechanical gate at the base of the private hill, mind you. There was a guardhouse there, with two armed guards, and an actual hand-cranked tollgate, which had to be moved to let us in. I noticed a pair of Harley-Davidsons parked by the tollgate. I guessed in the event we decided to do a little gate-crashing, the armed guards would hop on their hogs and follow us with guns blazing.

The guards had our names, so we easily entered the inner sanctum. Up, up, up a winding road that made our long driveway seem minuscule. We were deposited on a hilltop that towered over our own—I could see our house from there—in front of a sprawling white mansion. No, not a mansion. Mansion would mean one building. This was not a mansion. This was part of a compound, with various buildings splayed out on the hillside below us. They were all inspired by the main house, with soaring Greek columns.

"Impressive." Chad was the first to speak.

"Who buys a place like this?" my dad murmured.

"Someone with conspicuous consumption disorder?" I suggested.

"Please," Gemma snorted, and adjusted the neckline of

her pink T-shirt to show as much cleavage as she thought she could get away with. "*I'd* buy it if *I* could afford it."

Mom smiled. "Are you *sure* you're the kid of a minister?"

My dad craned around and motioned for Gemma to readjust her neckline to something more modest, which she did with a dramatic sigh.

"Welcome, Sheltons, welcome!"

Kent, Joan, Lisa, and their golden retriever, who we soon learned was named Jensen, after Kent's favorite sports car, bounded out to greet us. They looked like the ideal family. Kent was six two, young-looking for his fifty-five years, and wore a white tennis shirt and khakis. His thick salt-and-pepper hair seemed to glow in the late-afternoon light. Joan was about ten years younger, with the body of a woman who spent as much time being personally trained by Billy Blanks (the Stevens's home gym proved to rival Reebok's, and I am only slightly exaggerating) as going to charity board meetings. She wore an almost-too-short denim skirt and a blue silk short-sleeved shirt. Lisa was in a floral skirt the size of a Post-it and a red cami layered over a white cami. My sister eyed Lisa's impressive exposed cleavage and yanked her shirt lower again.

Let me see if I can get the grand tour of the Stevens estate down to two paragraphs, because if you're really interested, you can Google Earth it and get the aerial view. The main mansion had eleven bedrooms and ten baths. There were three guesthouses, a garage that had space for twenty cars, a stable with four Arabian horses, the aforementioned gym, and a small observatory with a thirty-inch reflecting telescope that pretty much let you look in the window of anyone who lived within twenty miles of the Big Dipper.

The thing that got me, more than anything else, was that the Stevenses had an art gallery. Actually, an art museum, which focused on late twentieth-century works by such artists as Jean-Michel Basquiat, Keith Haring, and Jeff Koons. One piece that really caught my eye was a dead shark suspended in an aquarium of formaldehyde. Kent told my dad and me—he was shepherding us around, with Lisa, Gemma, and Chad on our tail and my mother paired with Joan behind them—that the artist was Damien Hirst and he'd had to bid against dozens of others to acquire it.

Who'd buy such a thing? I could see a live shark in a big tank, maybe. If you were into hammerheads. But dead? Please. *That's* art?

Kent must have seen me looking at it askance. "Not your taste, Nat?"

Embarrassing.

I recovered quickly. "It's . . . interesting. I'm kind of more into French impressionists."

Kent smiled kindly. "We have a few of those, too, up in our bedroom. A Monet, a Manet, a Degas. Maybe after we sit a little, I'll take you up there." He motioned with his chin toward a small round table with a white tablecloth and several wooden stools whose blond wood matched that of the gallery floor. There was a bottle of champagne chilling in a bucket nearby and three silver-topped serving dishes on the table.

"Not a meal," Kent assured us. "That's later. Just an appetizer."

The moment we moved toward the table, a uniformed African American guy who looked like the model Tyson, only shorter, moved toward it, too. Where he'd been waiting, I had no idea. Once Gemma had caught up, she looked up at him from under her eyelashes, coated with, like, three layers of mascara. Honestly. My sister's T-shirts should all read *I flirt, therefore I am.*

"This is Keith," Joan said as the impossibly handsome guy lifted the tops off the serving dishes. "We'd all be lost without him."

"Thank you, Joan," Keith replied in a deep, melodious voice. He gestured to each plate as he uncovered it. "Cold lobster. Foie gras. Eight cheeses from eight countries in Europe. Enjoy." He disappeared silently from the room.

"Sit, sit, please," Joan urged us.

As we sat, Kent expertly opened the champagne.

"Charlie? May Nat partake? It's Taittinger. My personal favorite." Kent indicated my champagne flute.

My sister looked furious that the offer hadn't been extended to her, and my father looked flustered. In Minnesota, no one asked parents whether they could pour their underage kids champagne.

I bailed my father out. "I don't drink, Mr. Stevens."

"Kent," he said quickly. "Please, call us Kent and Joan. And good for you," he added approvingly. He cocked his head toward a bucket of ice in which canned soft drinks were nestled. "Help yourself, kids."

"I'd rather have the champagne, Daddy," Lisa said with a little-girl pout.

"Seriously," Gemma agreed quickly.

Mom eyed Gemma. "Seriously *not*," she said firmly.

"I read this article that said kids in families who don't make a big deal about alcohol are less likely to become alcoholics," Chad said.

Lisa smiled at him through her bubble gum pink lip gloss and crossed her smooth, tanned legs so that her tiny skirt rode up even farther. My little brother's eyes were glued to those gams. I wanted to remind Lisa that my little brother might look sixteen but he was all of thirteen. As in, his very first year of being an actual *teenager*. Then I figured Lisa was probably the L.A. version of Gemma. That is, she flirted because she could.

We chatted amicably about what we'd done in L.A. so far. When I told Kent that I'd been to the Hollywood Forever Cemetery to see a movie, he laughed with appreciation and then grinned at my father.

"You'd better stick with your daughter, Charlie. She'll show you how to enjoy Los Angeles. What have you been doing for fun?"

My dad shook his head ruefully. "Mostly trying to finish my new book. It's due at the publisher in sixty days."

Kent took a long sip of champagne. "That's right," he recalled. "You're a writer. A real writer, who writes books. Unlike all these hacks out here who claim to write, when they're actually banging out scripts."

"I wouldn't go that far," my dad said modestly.

"What's the title? What's it about?" Kent seemed truly interested.

"Well, it's a mystery."

"I love mysteries!" Kent exclaimed. "They make good movies. Are you going to tell me the plot? And the title?"

My father grinned, clearly happy that our host was showing such interest. "It's called *Inside Doubt*. Basically what happens is that this girl gets a heart transplant—"

"How old?" Kent interrupted.

"About twenty-five," I chimed in, wanting to be part of the conversation. I'd read the first half of the manuscript. It was really good.

"Excellent." Kent took another sip of champagne. "Very castable. Go on. What's it about?"

My dad traded a look with my mom, who nodded her encouragement. "I have a very talented husband," she put in helpfully.

Dad put his appetizer plate on the table. "It's a pretty simple story. This girl, Dru, she gets a heart transplant. Then she starts getting all these weird vibes and thoughts, like something is up with the heart donor. It's like the heart is speaking to her—'Help me! Help tell my story!'"

Kent was rapt. "Go on. I want to hear more."

My father's eyes got wide like they did whenever he was excited. "I don't want to give too much away."

"Talk, man!" Kent banged the table gently. "No one in this town reads, including me. Just tell me your story."

"Okay, okay," my dad said quickly. "Anyway, Dru sets out to find the person who gave her the heart—to find out how that person died. And what looks like an accident doesn't really have anything to do with an accident. He was murdered. The murderer figures out what she's doing, sees his cover being blown, and sets out to kill her, too."

"I love that!" Joan exclaimed, smoothing her already perfectly smooth hair.

"That's fantastic! How about Natalie Portman as the girl, Matt Damon as the guy who donates the heart, and maybe De Niro as the leader of the criminal gang that killed Damon in the first place?" Kent's eyes shone. This was clearly his element.

There was no criminal gang. Which is what my dad told Kent. In response, the producer chuckled. "Aw, we won't let that stop us. Listen, Charlie. Does anyone have an option yet on *Inside Doubt?*"

"What's an option?" Gemma asked breathlessly, clearly excited by all the movie talk.

"It gives a producer the right to produce a book or a script," Lisa explained, the showbiz-savvy kid that she was. She smiled at my brother again.

"My kid has the business in her blood," Kent said approvingly. "So this option, it's usually a small payment—maybe ten thou—to be followed by a larger payment if the movie actually gets written and shot, and a humongous payment if the movie gets released."

I could see my dad trying to stay cool. And failing. He cleared his throat. "My book hasn't been optioned."

"You control the rights?" Kent's eyes bored into his.

"Yes, I think—"

"Then send the manuscript—whatever you've got—to my office tomorrow. I'm interested. Correction: I'm really, really interested. This sounds like it would make a helluva movie, and I know exactly the right writer for it. Shane Black. Ever heard of him?"

I hadn't. Neither had my father. Kent told us to Google him and then stood.

"Well, this has been a productive get-together," he declared. "How about if we go out back for the real meal?"

Kent and Joan led the way. Gemma and Lisa walked together, whispering and giggling like old friends. Chad followed, his eyes on Lisa's thighs.

I caught up to my mom and dad. "Dad, that's so fantastic!"

Mom took Dad's hand. "It really is, Charlie."

"It's kind of amazing," Dad admitted, flushed with happiness. "I guess this is how people do things here."

I was thrilled for my dad. I really was.

Dinner was astonishing.

The Stevenses' huge back deck had an African theme. The teak flooring had been imported from Tanzania, the handcrafted furniture from Niger and Malawi, the native rugs from Botswana, and dotting the deck were pedestals of central African folk art. The meal was from French-speaking North Africa, set out on a long crafted table with a carved chair for each of us. There was spiced lamb barbecue from Morocco, heaping dishes of couscous, moussaka, Egyptian tablich zucchini, shish kebab; the food kept coming and coming, accompanied by a choice of wine or fragrant fruit juices. Kent and Joan were the perfect hosts, making us all feel part of the conversation. Kent even invited us to a future tour of the shooting set of his most successful TV show, *Working Stiff*, about a massage therapist who doubled as a private eye.

"Who knows?" He looked directly at Gemma, who'd expressed her interest in acting. "Maybe we can even find a part for you."

Gemma looked like she had died and was sitting in the lap of Our Heavenly Father, who was expounding about the boutiques in heaven before he handed her a no-limit black American Paradise Express card—*Don't leave your cloud without it.* "You mean it?"

"Gemma, as you get to know me," Kent said, "you'll come to see I never say anything I don't mean."

"I can vouch for that," Joan chimed in. "He asked me to marry him and didn't give me a choice."

Before dessert came out, Chad and Lisa said they were going up to the main house to play some pool in the rec room. The rest of us talked some more; my mother outlined some of her ambitious plans for the church while Kent nodded approvingly, and then we all walked down to a koi pond below their deck to feed the carp. We came back to a dessert of homemade ice cream, and finally it was time to go home. I volunteered to go up to the main house to get Chad.

I didn't find him in the rec room. Instead, I found him upstairs. In Lisa's room. They were shoulder to shoulder, flipping through her huge CD collection, laughing and exclaiming over bands they both loved and bands they both hated.

"Chad?" I asked.

He turned. "Oh, hey, Nat."

Lisa looked up at me, totally cool and in control. "Your brother has great taste in music."

I truly did not think my parents would be thrilled to find Chad where he was at that moment. But maybe I was over-reacting. Chad hadn't had a girlfriend yet. It wasn't his fault he looked so much older than he really was.

Chad thanked Lisa, and she walked us down to my family. There were more warm goodbyes, please-come-backs, and a reminder to my dad to send that manuscript to Kent. That was great. But all the way home, I wondered about Lisa Stevens and my brother. Then I decided I was reading too much into it. Definitely.

Chapter Nine

In the aftermath of our non-conversation about feelings, Sean and I kept our long-distance relationship going.

It wasn't hard. I emailed him every night with the news of the day. When I was invited to the set of *Working Stiff* on the following Friday, I told him. When I thought maybe I should get a job for the summer because it might be a good idea to try to earn some money of my own, but didn't know what that job should be, I told him. After a particularly good meeting with the church youth group, where we made plans with Mr. Bienvenu for an interfaith charity project, I told him.

We talked on AIM. We Skyped every other day or so. We traded a lot of texts. It was almost like it had been before we went to ground at the lake cabin, when things were uncomplicated and we kept it simple.

It wasn't all simple, though. There were several times when I tried to reopen the conversation about our feelings—to share how I was doing emotionally here as a stranger in a strange land. Sean couldn't really reciprocate. He managed to say that he was still planning to come to Los Angeles in July, that he missed me, and that I should be careful with all the crazy kids in Los Angeles. "Stick with the church and I think you'll be fine. Otherwise, who knows?" he warned.

That warning was why I didn't tell him everything. I didn't talk about my new friend Alex Samuels, fresh out of rehab. I definitely didn't talk about how I'd met a guy named Brett exactly once but thought about him a lot. I didn't talk about how, on Wednesday, I was having the first spa day of my life, courtesy of my new friend Alex.

"You're going on Friday to a TV set? You can't. Not with your hair like that," Alex had declared when we were walking together on the asphalt strip that everyone called the Venice Beach boardwalk. By the time we'd finished a breakfast of spinach and feta cheese omelettes at the Rose Café and Market, serenaded by a street musician doing Beatles covers, Alex had booked appointments for us at Agua Spa at the Mondrian hotel in West Hollywood.

Okay. I felt a little guilty when I did my online homework and took a look at the price lists. Their website had a menu of services and products: An hour of table shiatsu for $165. A revive/cellulite detox for $175. The Ultimate Manicure at $65. It was too much. I screwed up my courage and told Alex that I couldn't accept such an overly generous gift. She laughed and said she wouldn't mind paying, but the fact was that spas, hotels, and restaurants sent gift certificates to the homes of celebrities and club kids all the time so they could brag to other clients that such-and-such was a customer, or that so-and-so was expected to be in later in the afternoon. That day's treatments at Agua were courtesy of Agua. If there was anyone to thank, it was the Mondrian management. Which I was quite ready to do when an older but nimble Japanese woman worked on my nude back and thighs while I lay on a cedar-scented massage table. Six feet away from me, Alex was getting the same treatment from her own masseuse.

"Are we happy campers?" Alex asked, turning her head toward me. Her voice carried over soft Japanese music playing through the sound system.

"Blissful," I reported as the masseuse began to knead the tension out of my shoulders with oil that smelled of night-blooming jasmine.

Alex smiled and closed her eyes. "Good. There's a lot more spas where this one came from."

"This one is fine for me," I told her, and then was gently shushed by my masseuse.

"You need more relax," she told me quietly. "You carrying lots of tension, blocking good chi."

Figuring I needed all the good chi I could get, I closed my eyes and gave myself to the experience. Ahead of me, I knew, were a manicure, pedicure, hairstyling, and professional makeup application. Plus lunch at one of the hotel restaurants. Alex told me that plenty of people came to the Mondrian spa and then took a room upstairs because they didn't want the day to end.

Okay. I was loving it. I was feeling a teensy bit guilty about loving it, like how could it be fair for me to be so privileged when kids in L.A. were going hungry or their schools were filled with graffiti and they didn't even have their own textbooks? Not that giving up my massage was going to get them new textbooks. But still.

I was also thinking about why Alex had picked me to be her friend. I mean, it wasn't like she was lacking for fascinating human companionship. She knew tons of people. While I realized that she probably didn't want to surround herself with the same people she'd been hanging out with when she went into rehab, it couldn't be that every single one of her pre-rehab friends would fail a urine test. This was just a guess on my part. What about Brett?

Anyway, back to Alex. Was I a friend of convenience, because I lived within walking distance? Someone who wasn't a drinker or a druggie, who wouldn't tempt her to do something she'd later regret? Some kind of a project, like in the movie *Clueless* (which, by the way, if you've never seen it, you totally need to find), where I was the hick girl from Minnesota who she could help transform into Los Angeles beautiful, and this spa day at the Mondrian was just another step in that process?

No. That was just nuts. A day at Agua was par for the course for someone like Alex. She liked me; I liked her. Why wouldn't she invite me, especially if she wasn't paying for it? This was her normal, the same way that going to Salon De Lovely out on the Blue Earth Highway, where Mary Teegarden had been cutting my hair—my whole family's hair, for that matter—for as long as I could remember, was my normal. Alas, Mary didn't do shiatsu.

Agua shiatsu gave way to the mani/pedis, during which my

toes were done with robin's egg blue toenail polish. The nail tech gave me a foot massage that lasted almost a half hour before she went to work on the nails themselves. The manicure was fabulous—ballet pink polish, while Alex opted for steel gray.

After that, we were escorted down a short hallway to the Agua Spa hair salon. The salon also had a Zen vibe going on, all white on white with soft lighting that could be adjusted as necessary. Instead of the eighties hair metal I was used to hearing at Salon De Lovely, we were treated to Bach harpsichord. Alex and I were separated—there were neat partitions so clients didn't have to feel they were being watched by other clients—and I was taken under the wings of two more Japanese women, Yoko and Suki. Yoko was in charge; Suki did whatever Yoko wanted her to do. Yoko studied me from every angle. She lifted my hair and rubbed it between her fingers, let it fall against my neck, and pronounced my need for hair extensions.

Hair extensions? Like . . . sewing someone else's hair onto your hair and wearing it? So not me.

"You try," Yoko insisted. "If you don't like, I take off."

She had a point. So for nearly two hours, I closed my eyes and rode on the harpsichord as Suki and Yoko made the world's tiniest braids and then used some kind of tool to attach endless tiny bundles of incredibly gorgeous human hair, in shades of dark golden blond, and pale gold, to my own boring blondish locks. Yoko had me turned away from the mirror so I couldn't see what she was doing. Even after she finished the extensions, she used two different colors on just a few of the strands of my own hair in the front and at the crown, covering each one with tin foil while it "cooked."

"Looking good!"

I turned. There was Alex, still wearing one of the Mondrian-monogrammed white bathrobes we'd put on after our shiatsu. Her stylist had taken maybe two inches off her lush dark hair and had given her eye-grazing bangs.

"You look fantastic," I told her.

"Thanks." She cocked her head at the aluminum foil bundles on my head. "And you look like you could contact Mars," she teased.

A half hour later, when my hair had been rinsed and shampooed with something that smelled like fresh mint, then blown dry—with my back still to the mirror—Yoko finally pronounced me done and spun my chair around.

Holy whoa. I looked *so* good. The subtle variations in color brightened up my face, and the fantastic blow-out, away from my temples with some volume on top, made it look less round.

Yep. No doubt about it. Five hours after arriving at the salon, now massaged, mani'd, pedi'd, and hair extended, I was at least 20 percent cuter. Not Gemma cute. But still. No wonder people did this on a regular basis. I believe what came out of my mouth was:

"Wow."

"You like?" Yoko asked.

"I love," I admitted.

"You're not done. Makeup next, with Amber. Then, lunch. Because frankly, I'm starved." Alex smiled at me approvingly. "Wait till your sister sees you."

"She'll want to come here."

"She'll have to have a friend of her own take her," Alex declared. "Of course, Lisa Stevens probably lives here, so she's halfway home. But whatever. Let's get your makeup done."

Makeup turned out to be a fairly protracted affair, far more protracted than I would ever do in front of my own mirror. First there was Amber—tall, skinny, liberally tattooed—who, when I told her I had never had my eyebrows "done," looked as shocked as if I'd told her I didn't shower on a regular basis. She set to work plucking and grooming them into delicate arches. Then she applied makeup with a subtle hand: some luminous stuff on my skin that she assured me had a built-in sunscreen, Nars blush in a color called Orgasm—no, I don't know what they do for a marketing campaign—Dior eye shadow that made my eyes look bigger and brighter, tons of Dior mascara, and a peachy nude lip gloss that looked like my own natural lips, only a zillion times better.

When Amber finished, the person looking back at me from the makeup mirror was not even the new me post-extensions. It was an even cuter, way hotter version of me.

"Bye-bye, Mankato," Alex commented, her gaze meeting mine in the mirror.

I wasn't sure how I felt about her saying that. Did enjoying all this attention, all the primping, mean I was giving up my essential self and turning into someone I didn't know and might not even like just to fit in?

No. I would never be *that* girl.

"Come on." Alex tugged me out of the makeup chair. "Let's show you off."

The Asia de Cuba restaurant at the Mondrian was dazzling. The maitre d' took us to the outdoor patio, which held rows of four-seat white-clothed tables between rows of the biggest planter pots I'd ever seen—fully six feet high and five feet around, planted with ficus trees and bougainvillea bushes. I felt positively dwarfed.

"Alex! What a surprise!"

The voice came from between two of the planters just as we were about to sit. A moment later, Alex's friend Brooke squeezed through to talk to us. She looked even more amazing than she had the night we'd met at the cemetery, in a low-cut white tank tucked into a tiered high-waisted floral print skirt and platform espadrilles. After a big hug for Alex and a more modest one for me, plus an explanation that she was here with a couple of people whose names meant nothing to me, she stepped back and gave me an assessing look. "Someone pulled their look together. Nicely done."

"Thank you," I said politely.

"It really is an improvement, though it's gonna cost a fortune to keep the extensions up," she mused, lifting a handful of my hair, then letting it flutter back down against my cheek. "The makeup, too."

"Well, I probably won't do this all the time," I admitted. "It's a lot of work I can't afford."

I liked myself for saying that aloud. You can take the girl out of Mankato, but I didn't *want* to take the Mankato out of the girl.

"Shame," Brooke commented, oozing faux sincerity. Her gaze flicked ever so subtly to my thighs, then back to my face.

113

"You might want to start with a personal trainer, though. I have this guy that can give you buns of steel in like three weeks. In your case, though, I'd book him for the three-month special. Alex can give you my number. Gotta run. Alex, call me."

As fast as she'd shown up, she was off.

"Charm challenged," Alex decreed as we sat down and a handsome Latino waiter poured us glasses of springwater fragrant with orange slices.

No kidding.

"She can be a bitch." Alex sipped her water. "I think she's having a hard time with me being friends with you."

"I'm not like your other friends, you mean."

Alex shrugged. "You are who you are. I like you. That's good enough for me. It had better be good enough for them."

We ordered our lunches—lobster pot stickers and barbecued salmon for Alex (though she insisted that we share), and a grilled-chicken salad for me. While we waited for the food to arrive, Alex kept me entertained with stories about her friends. Nothing truly gossipy, just the various machinations of who had been whose boyfriend or girlfriend when. The couplings and decouplings were truly dizzying. I found myself hanging on every word, waiting for her to talk about Brett Goldstein. When she didn't, I polished off a pot sticker and then oh-so-casually asked about him.

"So . . . Brett seems nice," I ventured.

Alex grinned. "Does 'nice' mean 'hot' in Minnesota?" She forked a piece of salmon into her mouth.

"Nice *and* hot," I clarified, hoping I wasn't blushing.

"And taken," Alex reminded me. "Not that you should let a little detail like that stop you."

"I am not a boy poacher. Besides, his girlfriend, Skye, is six kinds of gorgeous. And sweet, too."

Alex raked a hand through her lush hair. "Sometimes. They haven't been together for very long. This time, anyway. I have this theory. When a new relationship is at its hottest, it has nowhere to go but down. I think Brett and Skye reached peak heat a month ago. Which means they're probably, like, two weeks away from breaking up."

"Come on," I chided. "Relationships are about more than sex."

Alex gave me a wide-eyed look. "Really?" Then she burst out laughing. "Okay, sometimes they are," she admitted. "But come on. Brett has like forty-eight IQ points on her. I don't think we're talking a meeting of the minds here."

So Brett was smart. I had kind of suspected that. Yet he chose to hook up with a gorgeous, sweet, but not too bright girl for the obvious reason. Which meant he was superficial. Which meant—

"You're still thinking about him," Alex said accusingly, digging back into her salmon. It had been pan-seared and was crusted with sesame seeds.

"No I wasn't," I said quickly. Correction: *lied* quickly.

"You have to try this fish. It's to die for." Then she mentioned a concert at the Hollywood Bowl later in the summer, Adele and Janelle Monáe, and asked whether I might want to go. I definitely did. I'm a huge Adele fan.

It made me think that I ought to invite her to something, too. The next night, at sunset, there would be a songwriters' night at the church, where several Oscar-winning songwriters would be performing their music, accompanied just by guitar or piano. It would take place in the courtyard, with refreshments and casual seating. These songwriters' nights were a church tradition. There was no charge, but there was a donation box for a worthy charity. The next event was raising money for Kidsave, a nonprofit organization that supported abandoned kids in Colombia, Russia, and Africa.

Maybe she'd like to go with me?

I asked.

She scowled. "Absolutely, positively not."

Whoa.

"You don't like that kind of music?"

Her face got two more shades of dark, like a fast-approaching summer thunderstorm. "The music is fine." Her voice was cold. "I just don't like churches."

"This isn't religious—"

"I know that," she said, cutting me off. "I'm not dense. But churches are not something I do, period. And don't ask me if I believe in God, because the jury is out on that one. I'm just not coming to your church. Period. End of discussion. Please don't ask me again."

That took me by surprise. Alex had been to rehab and seemed committed to her recovery. Many rehab programs are based on the Twelve Steps of Alcoholics Anonymous, which is a God-centered program. I know this because our church in Mankato frequently hosted Twelve Step meetings. Where were her meetings if they weren't in churches, and how could she do her recovery if the jury was out on the subject of God?

Besides, I hadn't invited her to just any church. I'd invited her to my church, where my mother was the minister—the same mother who had not called the cops when her brother decided my bedroom was the ideal location for a naked guitar recital. And I wasn't asking her to come for Sunday worship, or any kind of worship. It was a songwriters' night!

I felt hurt. Here I was, accepting Alex for who she was and accepting her past. Church was part of my past; it was part of my present and my future, too. It was as much a part of me as breathing. Who was Alex to declare she would never set foot in one? It wasn't like her prescription for living had been all that effective.

Then I thought about Sean and me. It wasn't like my prescription for living had been 100 percent effective, either.

I considered challenging Alex anyway but then remembered something my mother had once preached in our Mankato church. "When it comes to matters of God, religion, and our church family, we attract more people by what we do in five seconds than by any words we could speak in an hour."

As I recalled my mom's sermon, Alex reached under the table for a small bag from the spa. She thrust the bag at me. "For you. Open it."

"You didn't need to—"

She held up a hand to stop me. "Please don't do the sputtering oh-I-can't-accept-it thing. What good is a makeover if you can't keep it up?"

I opened it, and there inside were all the cosmetics that had been used to create my new and improved face. She must have bought them while I was in the makeup chair. I fingered the gorgeous Dior lip gloss tube, with its gold crested crown. It was a little work of art. How would I ever return to CoverGirl or Maybelline or whatever was on sale at the drugstore?

"I don't know what to say," I murmured, glad I'd held my tongue before. "It's so generous."

"No biggie," Alex insisted. She changed the topic to clothes and some of the boutiques near the hotel she wanted to show me.

I listened, thinking about the opposites. Alex had such a strong, negative reaction to the idea of coming to church, and then she turned around and gave me this amazing gift. I had a feeling there was a lot I still didn't know about my new friend, and possibly a lot that she didn't want me to know.

Chapter Ten

"Ladies and gentlemen, friends of the Church of Beverly Hills, let's give a big hand to Mr. Kenny Loggins!"

Kent Stevens, dressed in Hollywood-chic black jeans, a white T-shirt, and a black sport coat, swept his hand toward the singer-songwriter with the scruffy beard and expressive brown eyes. The audience of five hundred rose to their feet and cheered as Kenny unstrapped his guitar and took a sheepish bow.

Gemma leaned toward me. "He's so *old*."

"He's fantastic," I declared.

Kenny had just run through a medley of some of his biggest hits, from "House at Pooh Corner" to "Your Mama Don't Dance," and then segued into songs he'd written for classic movies like *Top Gun* and *Footloose*. I knew the tunes but didn't know that Kenny had been the songwriter. I admit to a fleeting moment of jealousy. What a life that had to be.

Wake up, hang around, maybe go to the gym or walk your dog, come home, write a song, get that song in a movie, and then hear your song every time you saw the film.

Kent slung a friendly arm around Kenny. "Kenny's not going anywhere," he announced. "But he could use a break. Let's go to the social hall for dessert, and come back shortly for the second half of our show."

The crowd applauded this, too, and I couldn't help thinking that if Alex had come with me, she would have had a fantastic time. In addition to Kenny Loggins, we'd heard from Alicia Keys. After the refreshments and more numbers from Kenny, Matt Redman was supposed to close the show. It was a lineup that people would have paid hundreds of dollars a ticket to hear, if they could get a ticket. But if you were a member of the Church of Beverly Hills, you could come to hear them for free. I figured that it was partly out of the goodness of these artists' hearts, and it was partly because their agents, their managers, their lawyers, and the chief executives of the movie companies that had made the movies in which their songs had been featured were sure to be in the audience. It really didn't matter what motivated the musicians. The clear plastic collection box for Kidsave was at the entrance to the courtyard, and by the time I'd arrived, it was already full of cash and checks.

It was a night of great music. The courtyard had been set up with risers and chairs in a neat semicircle around the stage, almost like theater in the round. No expense had been spared; professional lighting towers rose dozens of feet in the air, and a first-class sound system had been erected. It was as different from my coffeehouse experience in Minnesota, where

I sometimes played my own songs, as my church here was different from my church in Mankato. I know. I'd been in Los Angeles for a week now. I should have been used to it. But I wasn't used to it, and I wasn't sure that I could ever get used to it.

I was sitting with Gemma a couple of rows from the stage, while my parents were in the front. Chad, unfortunately, had to miss it, since his new swim coach was working him out at the UCLA pool. He would come to the church when he was done; maybe he could catch the end of Redman's set.

The crowd filed out for intermission, buzzing good-naturedly, while Gemma searched for Lisa and a bunch of her friends. I waited for the aisle to clear before I stepped down, wondering if I should call Alex to say that maybe this was the one night when she should have gotten over her I-don't-do-church thing.

I felt a hand on my shoulder as I joined the throng moving to the social hall. "Nat! Hi!"

I turned. There was Sandra, wearing a pair of black pants and a purple T-shirt from the church youth mission to the Gulf Coast of Mississippi last summer, where they'd helped with the ongoing oil-spill cleanup. I was dressed just as casually, in cutoff jeans and a shirt from the Minnesota State Fair.

"Hey, how goes it?" I said.

She stared at me. "Oh my gawd. You look amazing! What did you do?"

I felt myself blush. I wasn't used to being complimented on my appearance and I knew she wasn't talking about my couture.

"Your hair is amazing. And the makeup. Boy, you sure took to L.A. fast."

I swallowed hard. I was going to tell the truth, even if it

killed me. "Alex took me to Agua Spa at the Mondrian. She had a gift certificate. It was my first spa day ever."

Sandra pursed her lips. "Well, it worked."

I waited, sure that some snarky comment about Alex would follow. But it didn't. Instead, Sandra steered me around a clump of people who had gathered to chat in the middle of the lobby. Three minutes later, we were in the social hall. Although I was used to the church's pulling out all the stops when it came to food, the "dessert" Kent had mentioned was still eye-popping. There were three long—I mean, twenty yards long—tables covered by red-and-white-checked tablecloths. On them was arrayed an astonishing assortment of baked desserts, plus a gelato bar, plus a dessert crepe-or-Russian-blintz station manned by a French chef.

Sandra and I joined the crepe line, where the chef was turning out chocolate and strawberry crepes almost as fast as he could pour the batter on his eight-burner griddle. "So Alex Samuels took you to the spa."

I should have known that conversation wasn't over. "Yep."

"Did she offer you cocaine?"

Sheesh.

"Of course not. For one thing, I don't do drugs and Alex knows it. For another, she just got out of rehab."

Sandra rubbed her nostrils for emphasis. "I take it you did your homework about her."

"I read a few things, yeah. And I talked to her. Yes. She had some problems in the past."

Sandra hooted. "Problems in the past? Natalie, I got a D in algebra. That's a problem in the past. I—yes, it's true—I got into my parents' vodka with a couple of friends when I was in ninth grade. That's a problem in the past. I drove my parents' Beamer to the beach before I had my license. That's a problem in the past. Compared to Alex, they should nominate me for sainthood." She put a hand on my arm again. "Just watch yourself, okay?"

I was getting kind of sick of hearing that. "Sure. Got it."

"How come she isn't here?" Sandra asked suddenly. "Did you invite her?"

I nodded. "She didn't want to come. She isn't that much into churches."

"She isn't that much into churches," Sandra echoed. "Why am I not surprised?"

We reached the service area and gave our orders to the chef. Sandra wanted one with chocolate; I wanted one of each. The chef—a mustachioed guy with a strong nose and the bushiest eyebrows I'd ever seen, but still very cute—grinned at me. "Two! Two crepes! You are ze first woman of ze night to ask for two! Ze American girls, zey eat nothing. Will you marry me?"

I grinned, and even Sandra cracked a smile. "I'll live dangerously," she chimed in. "Two for me, too."

We shared a smile. I liked her, but I didn't feel connected the way I felt connected to Alex. With Alex, I felt like I had a friend who was letting me gaze into her soul, and who didn't let all that many people in. It made me feel special.

As we took our white ceramic plates—the crepes looked amazing—and started hunting for a place to sit, I saw a girl our age standing by the doors that led to the main sanctuary beyond. She was petite, probably not taller than five feet, with dreadlocks past her shoulders and smooth skin the color of café au lait. Her huge eyes were set in a high-cheekboned, heart-shaped face. She wore black capris and an aqua embroidered peasant shirt. She looked nervous.

Now, I should say that the membership of the Church of Beverly Hills is heavily white, though I had seen a few black and Latino families in the pews the past Sunday. That may not seem like much, but our church in Mankato had exactly zero members of color. Zero. That's Minnesota for you. Not that there weren't black families in Mankato, but they tended to attend churches on the other side of town. My mom had done a bunch of pulpit-exchange and youth group projects with those churches, the Baptist one especially. She'd already taken some steps in that direction here in Los Angeles. The upcoming interfaith soup kitchen at a park in the San Fernando Valley was just one example.

"Do you know her?" I asked Sandra, raising my chin to the African American girl I'd spotted.

"Can't say I do." Sandra shook her head and then waved across the crowded room. "There's Courtney and Gordon. Want to go hang with them?"

I did and I didn't. I needed to meet more people. That was for sure. The girl by the door was all alone. I glanced back. She was gone.

"Please, take my plate?" I asked Sandra. "I'll be back in a minute."

Sandra took my crepes, and I headed toward the doorway where the girl had been hanging out. I knew what it was like to be someplace where you didn't feel like you fit in.

She wasn't in the doorway. She wasn't in the hallway. I found her in the empty sanctuary, where she'd boldly flipped on the lights. She stood in the back and seemed lost in thought.

When my knee banged into a pew—a klutz moment—she turned around and saw me.

"Don't arrest me for church-busting," she said. "I'm innocent. I swear to God." She looked pointedly at the ceiling. "Isn't that right, God? If it is right, don't say anything."

I laughed. This girl—whoever she was—was *funny*.

She rubbed her chin thoughtfully. "Did you ever think that when you talk to God, it's called praying, but when God talks to you? That's called schizophrenia."

I laughed again. "Are you new here?"

"I'm new pretty much everywhere right now," she replied. "Mia." She held out a hand for me to shake.

"I'm Natalie. Natalie Shelton. I suppose I should tell you—you'll find out soon enough if you stay for more than five minutes—my mother is the new minister here. Are you a member?"

Mia shook her head. "No."

"How'd you get in, then?" I wasn't being the visitor police; I was genuinely curious.

"Oh, I didn't come for the concert. I had no idea it was going on."

"Then . . . ?"

"Church shopping. Checking it out. The lady at the door said it was fine for me to look around."

I grinned. "Impossible to say no to you, huh?"

She grinned right back. "It happens. Rarely."

"Why not come on a Sunday? You'll get the whole experience."

"Including your mother in action, no doubt." Mia stretched her arms overhead. "It can't be easy being the new girl at a new church with your mom as the minister. Hang in there. Anyway, I like to come during off-hours. Less conspicuous. And if the sermon sucks, I'm not trapped."

I mock-frowned at her. "My mom's sermons are actually good—please don't ever tell her I admitted that. She talks to people instead of lecturing."

"Then maybe I will come on a Sunday, sometime."

I felt bold. "Why don't you stick around for the second half of the concert? I'll sit with you. The music is great."

Mia shook her head. "Not tonight." She looked at her watch. "In fact, I should probably be going."

I wasn't ready to say goodbye to this girl. "One more option. This weekend we're doing a charity thing over in the San Fernando Valley—"

She laughed. "You're such a rookie! No one calls it the San Fernando Valley. It's just the Valley. Or, if you want to be cool, Natalie? Call it the eight one eight."

I must have looked blank.

"Area code. Eight one eight area code. That's where I used to live."

"Oh, so you moved, and that's why you're church shopping—"

"It's complicated." She folded her arms, body language that said, "Don't ask any more questions."

I told her about the interfaith soup kitchen thing. "There'll be a lot of kids from a lot of different churches. You could look at it as one-stop shopping."

She smiled. "Where are you from?"

"Minnesota."

She shrugged. "Never been."

"It's great," I said, and heard the wistful sigh in my voice.

"I'm sure you have tons of black friends there."

I could feel the color rush to my face.

"Minnesota is pretty . . . white."

"Well, you're in Los Angeles now," Mia pointed out. "Lots of people of color here. Every color and then some."

I nodded. "That's one of the things I like. But . . . it's all still so new to me. I mean . . . to tell you the truth? I don't feel like I really belong here."

Her eyes moved to my fab new and improved hair. "Well, your extensions sure do."

I touched my hair self-consciously. "You mean you can tell?"

"My mom used to do them for her friends," Mia explained. "I know all about weaves."

"Does your mom have a salon?"

Something in Mia's face closed down as the lights flickered, signaling that intermission was coming to an end. "You'd better get back to the concert."

"Sure you don't want to come with?" I offered.

"Hey, Natalie?" she said, dodging my question.

"Yeah?"

"For what it's worth . . . I don't feel like I belong here, either," she said softly, then pivoted out the door.

It wasn't until she was gone that I realized I didn't even know her last name.

Chapter Eleven

"Sound . . . and . . . action!"

My sister and I watched quietly from one side of the set of *Working Stiff,* my father and brother observing from the other side, as the assistant director—not the director, the way it always goes in the movies—called for the cameras to roll and the scene to begin.

The set was a mock-up of a basement massage studio far more Spartan than the one I had recently experienced with Alex at the Mondrian. The Mondrian massage room was upscale. This was definitely downscale, with only a massage table; an array of rough wooden shelves that held the tools of the trade, like oils and powders; and a folding chair, on which had been placed a small stack of Holiday Inn–grade white towels and white sheets. Except for a boom box and a single Zen-themed poster taped to the far wall, that was it.

It was the day after the concert. My family, with the

exception of my mother, who was working at the church, had accepted Kent Stevens's invitation to visit the Studio City production facility of his hit hour-long drama, *Working Stiff*.

Working Stiff had been on the air for two years, though I'd never watched it. It was about a middle-class Los Angeles woman named Shauna, who had a legitimate home massage-therapy office but moonlighted as a private investigator with an uncanny knack for cracking cases the police had deemed hopeless. I had watched a few YouTube clips to prep for this visit. To be honest, it wasn't my kind of show. I'm more old *Gilmore Girls, Secret Life,* and—sue me—classic *7th Heaven*.

Everything associated with the writing, shooting, and production of *Working Stiff* took place in a single nondescript five-story building on busy Riverside Drive in Studio City, in the 818 (Mia would be proud!), not far from the Fashion Mall. The show had taken over the building for the duration of its run. The aboveground part of the building held the show's interior sets, including the massage room, the messy home PI office, the apartment that belonged to the heroine and her teenage son, police headquarters, et cetera. Down in the basement, you could find the production offices, editing bays, and even the room where the writers would gather to map out new episodes.

Kent himself gave us a quick tour before he took us to watch the filming. I thought the writers' room was one of the most depressing places I'd ever seen. No windows, walls covered with whiteboards, and two conference tables that held the fallout of pizzas long forgotten. The room smelled of old perspiration, stale coffee and dead yeast, too little sleep, and too much anxiety. It was enough to make me decide never to pursue a career as a television writer. Who in their right mind would do that?

The shooting sets, though, were incredibly cool. Kent showed us how a particular room could be transformed by the crew in a couple of hours from one use to another, and there were other areas filled with props, false walls, and the like. The dressing rooms, makeup area, and hair stations were crowded with people who obviously loved their jobs. We even met the show's publicist, whose job it was to keep *Working Stiff* in the public eye.

The night before, Kent had messengered to our house the script for the day's shooting, with scenes marked with Post-it notes. He'd scrawled a message in longhand on the cover. "This'll help you understand better, Sheltons. Can't wait!"

He was right. Without that script, I would have been lost. The gist of the episode in progress was that Shauna's teen son—a guy named Zack—comes home to the apartment one day after playing basketball to make a shocking discovery: a good friend of his mother's is dead in their shared bathroom. The police suspect Shauna, but then suspicion falls on Zack himself. Shauna has to find the real killer so that Zack doesn't go to prison for life.

We were about to watch the scene in which Zack rushes into the massage room and announces to his mom that her friend Jodi is dead. This was the last scene in the "teaser," the part of the script that comes before the first commercial and makes people want to stay tuned instead of changing the channel to, say, *CSI*.

"Action!"

The assistant director repeated his call and we watched attentively as the lights turned hot and the scene got going. Shauna, who looked like Scarlett Johansson's older sister, except thinner, was kneading knots out of a client discreetly draped by a white sheet. They exchanged a little small talk about the kind of massage the client wanted: a happy ending. Shauna shut him right down. He'd have to find that at the Porn Palace downtown. Then there was a bang on the door to the massage room, and Zack burst in.

"Mom! It's Jodi! She's just lying there on the floor in a big pool of blood. . . . I think she's dead!"

As Zack delivered his lines with appropriate fear and upset, I almost fell on the floor. I knew the actor—not from seeing him on TV or reading about him in the tabloids, either. You may think this is bulldooky, but it's true: I'd had absolutely no idea who played Zack on *Working Stiff* until that very moment.

Brett Goldstein. Alex's friend. Skye's boyfriend. My . . . my nothing, except in occasional dreams.

"And . . . cut!" The assistant director ended the shooting and told his crew that they'd move on to the next scene after lunch. With that, a small army descended on the massage room to pack things up and tell the actors where they needed to go for the first sequence of the afternoon.

I was about to share with Gemma that I knew the actor playing Zack when Brett spotted me, his jaw going slightly slack in surprise. Then a broad smile spread over his sunny face. I was grateful that I'd been uncharacteristically vain that morning, giving my new extensions a thorough blow-out and applying my makeup as best as I remembered from Agua Spa. When I left the house, I thought I was looking fairly cute. I had on my favorite pair of jeans, blue flip-flops, and a sort of retro light blue blouse with yellow embroidery around the scooped neckline.

He waved. I waved back.

He waved more enthusiastically. I waved again.

"Oh my gawd," Gemma observed. "That actor? The cute one playing Zack? He's flirting with you!"

"I know him," I said softly.

"Oh shut the front door," Gemma scoffed. "You *know* him?"

I would have explained, except Brett threaded his way across the set toward us, a fact that was underscored by my sister's "Oh my gawd, he's coming over here!" and double hair flip with locks that never needed any extensions. Also by my skyrocketing pulse and blood pressure.

"Natalie? It's great to see you! What are you doing here?"

He put his arms out to me. What could I do? I hugged him. Okay. It's true. I liked the idea of hugging him in public. Especially in front of my sister, with her hair flips.

"I had no idea you were on this show," I told him when we let go of each other. Then I turned to my sister, who was looking at me with something new in her eyes. Something I'd never seen in them before. Something that would violate the tenth commandment. She was coveting the hug I'd just gotten from Brett Goldstein. "Gemma, this is Brett Goldstein. Brett, this is my sister, Gemma."

He put his hand out; she shook it, taking in his dark hair

132

and deep brown eyes. Still in his just-came-from-basketball costume for the scene—baggy gold gym shorts, beat-up Michael Jordan basketball shoes, and a Lakers jersey over a white T-shirt, he looked—and there were no two ways about it—hot. Hot hot.

"Hey, nice to meet you," he said easily.

"How do you know my sister?" Gemma managed to respond.

Brett smiled slyly. "Come on. She's been in town for what, a week now? Ten days? The whole city knows her. In fact, who doesn't know her?"

I grinned, Gemma looked at me askance, and then our attention was taken by a thin male voice from behind us.

"Gemma Shelton?"

A small guy as thin as his voice, with a bulging clipboard in his hands, had approached us. He had short sandy hair and was dressed more formally than anyone else on the set, in a sport coat, a white shirt, and black trousers. His ID badge identified him as Howie Lawrence, chief production assistant. It took all of thirty seconds to understand that Howie took his job very seriously.

"I'm Gemma Shelton," my sister told him.

Howie was nervous. "Gemma, Mr. Stevens wants to know if you have a moment to talk. He said to tell you he has something for you and his daughter, Lisa. In his office."

Gemma brightened. To be summoned by the show's executive producer was no small thing.

"Go," Brett instructed her. "Howie, can you make sure Gemma gets to Craft Service afterward?"

"Sure thing, Brett. Follow me, Gemma." Howie headed off, with my sister a few feet behind.

"Craft Service?" I asked. I had no idea what Brett was talking about.

He rolled his eyes in fake disbelief. "You really are FOB."

"FOB?" Baffled again.

"Fresh off the boat. FOB. Craft Service? It's what we call the people who serve us lunch. Even though it's still just"—he checked his watch—"ten-thirty. But the crew's been at it since five. Union rules, we take a break. Hungry? It's usually really good."

I was hungry, since hair washing, drying, and blowing had taken up a lot more time than I had planned. Time that I normally would have used to eat breakfast. "Sounds good to me."

"Excellent. Then it's a date."

Holy sugar on a shingle.

Brett Goldstein had just asked me out and accepted on my behalf. Sure, it was just lunch. Lunch at his place of work. Lunch that he hadn't been planning to ask me to join him for even fifteen minutes earlier. But—wait a sec. Skye. His girlfriend. Still. He'd asked me to lunch and I'd said yes. And here he was, holding his arm out for me to take.

What could I do, reader? With all due respect to Jane Austen: That arm, reader? I took it.

Of course, because that's the way my life works, that was the moment Sean chose to text me.

I stopped to check my cell, thinking that it might be Alex, who I hadn't seen in a couple of days, but who'd left a message the night before saying that she wanted to take a drive with me down to Redondo Beach for the sunset.

Nope. Not Alex. Just this:

Nat! Great news! Got refundable ticket!
Emailed tentative itinerary. See you soon!
Love xxx, SEAN

Chapter Twelve

Why did he have to do it that instant? Why couldn't he have just sent his email? Why did he have to ruin what Brett Goldstein had already called a date, even though I knew he had a girlfriend and he didn't know that I had a boyfriend?

"Everything okay?" Brett was watching me stare at my cell.

"Umm . . ." I looked up at him. "Crisis back in Minnesota with some friends," I invented.

Well, that wasn't a lie, exactly. Nor was it the truth, exactly. It was somewhere in between. Which made it immediately suspect.

"Something you need to handle right away? Can it wait till after lunch?"

I made a quick decision. "It can wait . . . ," I heard the hesitation in my voice.

"But you don't want it to," Brett said, as if he had read my mind. "Look, if there's someone you need to call, or you need to check your email in private or something, the script supervisor's office is on the way. He's probably at lunch already. Feel free."

"You sure it's okay?"

He laughed. "I'm an actor. I'm at the top of the food chain until they kill me off in a mysterious murder-by-massage-oil. Come on." He put his arm out again. "As long as no one is dying, it'll be okay."

Easy for him to say.

He was right about the script supervisor's office, though. It wasn't far and it had an actual door that closed, too. Brett ushered me inside. "I'll be out here."

"This shouldn't take long," I promised.

"Make it snappy." Then he laughed. "Seriously, take all the time you need." He closed the door behind him.

I checked my mail on the desktop. Sure enough, Sean's itinerary was the first item in new mail. I scanned it, heart pounding, and then breathed a little easier when I saw that he wouldn't be arriving for two whole weeks. Fourteen days, if it was okay with my folks. I'd been thinking that maybe he'd show up two days later or something.

I knew I had to write back. But what?

Here's what I wrote: "Great! In hurry so will keep it short. Will check dates with parents but I'm sure it'll be fine. Can't wait. Me."

Okay. That was a classic stall for time. Maybe if he was willing to talk about his feelings more, I'd be more excited about his coming to visit. I told myself that I had to give it one more try with him on the phone or Skype, at least. Maybe he could open up or read my emotions in my voice, the way Brett had when he suggested I come into this very room to deal with the mystery text.

"Everything okay?" Brett asked when I stepped back into the hallway.

"Crisis averted, no massage-oil murders," I assured him in my peppiest voice.

He laughed. "Great. We live to eat another day."

I expected that we'd end up in some sort of subbasement cafeteria, but Craft Services for *Working Stiff* was nothing of the sort. Brett led us outside, past an active loading dock, and then to a large multicolored tent behind the building with room for 150 people. Beyond the far end of the tent were three large catering trucks. People were lined up in front of each truck. Inside the tent, a long table held salads, another held cold drinks, another held sandwich-making gear, and yet another was reserved for desserts.

"Let's see what they're serving today," Brett said, my arm still looped through his. On an old-fashioned blackboard near the catering trucks, I read the offerings. Roasted shrimp with garlic. Skirt steak smothered in onions. Pasta with pesto sauce. And a non-peanut vegetarian alternative, a hearty potato and leek soup.

Okay. These people, on this show, ate really well.

As Brett and I joined the line at one of the catering trucks, he explained that great food for the cast and crew was a Hollywood tradition. Even if a star agreed to be in a low-budget movie for much less than their regular salary, they knew that when it came to meals and snacks, they'd be well taken care of. Same thing went for TV shows. It was also a tradition for everyone working on a production to eat together, even really big stars like Angelina Jolie or Katherine Heigl.

Katherine Heigl again. My twin, if you were, say, legally blind. I would like to say that I turned around just in time to see *the* Katherine Heigl step inside the *Working Stiff* Craft Services tent, but that would not be something between the truth and a lie. That would be an outright *lie*.

I ordered the shrimp, made myself a small spinach salad, got a bottle of mango juice, and sat down across from Brett at the end of one table. He'd ordered the steak and fries. He didn't have another scene to shoot until late in the afternoon. We had plenty of time to talk.

Yay.

Like Alex, Brett came from a Hollywood family, but one that was surprisingly stable compared to the cliché I had in my mind. His parents had met in film school at the University of Southern California and, after fifteen years, were still married to each other. Yes, this meant that Brett had been born two years before his parents got married. Don't be picky. This was Los Angeles.

His mother was better known than his father, since she ran one of the most famous showbiz blogs in the city, itsawraptinseltown.com. I'd never heard of it, but Brett assured me that along with Nikki Finke's deadlinehollywood.com, his mother's blog was a must-read for insider information. Who was hired, who was fired, what was being made, who had power, and who lost it—the blog covered it all. As for his father, he had left his prestigious Century City law firm ten years earlier to work for a tiny Internet start-up that delivered movie DVDs by mail and had expanded in the last few years into online streaming.

Netflix.

"That kinda worked out," Brett observed wryly. He cut a chunk of medium-done steak and popped it into his mouth.

"Good for the banking business?"

Brett gently bit his lower lip—a gesture I later came to learn meant that he felt uncomfortable with whatever he was talking about. "You have no idea."

"Do they give a lot away?" My parents always said that people who made a lot of money had a responsibility to give back to society.

"Well, there's a new Asperger's syndrome research facility at the neuropsychiatric institute at UCLA," Brett said. "My dad paid for it. Anonymously. He'd be pissed if he knew I told you. And they give a million a year to federation."

"Federation?" I had no idea what he was talking about.

"Jewish Federation. It's this big charity. They do that anonymously, too." Brett took a sip of Coke. "Yeah. They give a lot away. That doesn't mean we don't live conspicuously, though. We do. My mom has a thing for Rolls-Royces. She drives a different one every day of the week."

I laughed, thinking he was joking. His face told me that he wasn't.

"But . . . why?" I asked.

He shrugged and cut more steak. "Because she can."

"Well, I drive a Saturn," I told him. "An *old* Saturn. The same one. Every day."

"You rebel!" He smiled. "Who knows, maybe you'll start a trend. Though I don't see my friends flocking to Craigslist to buy used Saturns."

I tried my spinach salad, topped with fresh crumbled bacon and chunks of creamy blue cheese.

"Good, huh?" Brett asked.

"We don't get cheese like this in Mankato."

"It is good," he acknowledged. "But there are places in this town that make this taste like the high school cafeteria. Maybe I can show you sometime?"

He was asking me out on a real date.

But . . . what about Skye? And Sean? Fortunately or unfortunately, depending on how you feel about my lowering my ethical standards due to Hot Guy-itis, I didn't say any of that. Instead I said, "I'd like that."

"Hey, who wouldn't want to be seen with a such a beautiful girl?" His eyes bored into mine. "You do look great, you know. The air out here must agree with you."

Oh, so he liked my makeover. Maybe more than he liked the real me.

In my mind, I saw Skye the Beautiful, his supposedly significant other. If I was her, I wouldn't want my boyfriend asking the new girl from Minnesota to have dinner with him at some snazzy restaurant TBD. And Sean . . .

Maybe my concern showed on my face, because Brett beat me to the punch. "You're thinking about Skye?"

"Yeah," I admitted. "Aren't you guys . . . ?"

"We've got a—how can I put it?—unconventional relationship," he confided.

"Define 'unconventional.'" It sounded ominous.

"Well, we're the only ones who know this, but we have an arrangement. We're boyfriend and girlfriend, as long as one of us isn't interested in someone else. When one of us gets interested, we put us on ice for a while, and maybe forever."

The most intelligent response I could come up with was "Oh."

"She's fun," he continued. "She thinks I'm fun, and we both know the other isn't 'the one.' Call me crazy, but we've been doing it this way for two years." He made a face. "It must sound nuts. But we've always got someone to be with, when we're not with someone else. If we really and truly fall in love with other people? We're happy for each other."

That's what "unconventional" meant in L.A. Back in Mankato, we just called it "cheating." However, I wasn't in Mankato anymore.

But what if Brett wanted to take me out the night that Sean arrived? It could happen.

"So why don't you give me your cell—" Brett never finished his request. He was interrupted by Gemma, who came barreling up to our end of the table on a dead run, a stapled sheaf of papers in her right hand.

"Omigosh, omigosh!" She was shouting, and her eyes were shining. "Mr. Stevens just gave me a part in the show! Omigosh, omigosh!" She pointed at Brett. "With you!"

Brett handled the news with aplomb. "That's great. Why don't you sit down and tell us about it?"

Gemma did, the words spilling out so quickly she could have used a simultaneous translator. The English version of her babble was that there was a scene in which Shauna would be escorted out of her apartment by the police for questioning. Brett's character was going with her for moral support. Two teenagers who lived on the same floor would see this happening and would shout something to her. Originally, two professional actresses had been hired, but Kent Stevens had made a switch, paid the actresses but sent them home, and given the roles to his daughter and Gemma, with the possibility that they'd even appear in later episodes.

"What's your line for today, Gemma?" Brett's voice had a touch of gentle amusement.

Gemma looked down at the pages in her hand, a photocopy of the scene. "Let me see. . . . 'Good luck, Shauna!' That's it. 'Good luck, Shauna!'"

"I'm sure you'll nail it," Brett assured her. He rubbed his chin thoughtfully and cut his eyes to me for a split second before looking back at my sister. "I wonder if you might want a couple of tips."

"Tips? I'd love some tips!" Gemma gushed.

Brett turned to me again. "Would you excuse us for a moment? This is inside stuff, reserved only for working professionals."

How thoughtful. Out of the corner of my eye, I could see Gemma beaming.

"Sure. I'll get some ice cream."

"Make it a triple scoop," my sister suggested, batting her eyelashes at Brett. "Eat slow."

I stepped across the room toward the dessert table as Brett scraped his chair closer to my sister. On the way, I saw my brother with Lisa, their heads together over her iPhone as they looked at something and laughed. That was sweet. It was good to see him happy. Just before I got to the desserts, I spotted my dad sitting with Kent Stevens. He waved to me excitedly, beckoning me to join them. I held up a "one moment" finger, scooped a single serving of rum raisin ice cream into a dish, and then walked over.

"Sweetheart!" My father was upbeat. "It's so great to see you!"

"You're in a good mood," I told him, figuring that he was psyched that my sister was actually going to be on the show. "You heard what's happening with Gemma?"

"I did," he confirmed. "It's fantastic!"

"But that's not why he's so pumped up," Kent said. "Do you want to tell her, Charlie? Or should I?" Kent raised his eyebrows supportively, then looked at me. "I just gave your father some good news. Go on, Charlie. Tell her. It isn't bragging if it's true."

Dad put a hand on my shoulder. "Your father is now an optioned Hollywood writer. Kent took an option on *Inside Doubt*."

"Not me personally," Kent said. "Kent Stevens Productions." Then he grinned at me. "Your father's new book is going to be a major motion picture if I have anything to say about it." He swung back to my dad. "Congratulations again, Charlie. May it be the beginning of a long and prosperous relationship."

Impulsively, I hugged my father. "That is so great. That is so, so great. Does Mom know?"

My dad nodded. I'd never seen him look so happy. "She does. If she checks her voice mail."

"Which nobody does in this town," Kent observed. "So you two may have a chance to break the news when you get home. Of course, it's probably already on itsawraptinseltown.com." Then he wagged a finger at my father. "Now, don't you go getting some big agent at Paradigm and hold me up for a ton of money. Not until your second movie, at least."

My father laughed, and my cell sounded with another text.

Sean, I thought immediately. My stomach did a bad kind of flip-flop.

It wasn't Sean. It was a text that put the perfect coda on what had been a perfect day for the Shelton family so far, a text that confirmed to me and to any reasonable observer that we had done exactly the right thing by moving to Los Angeles.

It was from Brett.

Beautiful Natalie: Your sister gave me your digits. Now I've got yours and you've got mine. Let's plan that date. Brett.

Okay. It wasn't a movie option. And it wasn't even a bit part on a TV show. But I still levitated, and I defy anyone to tell me that I didn't.

Chapter Thirteen

"And here we have Big Jam's boudoir. This is where Big Jam kicks back."

The imposing black man with the shaved head—Big Jam himself—led an offscreen entourage into a marble-walled space roughly the size of a basketball court. He pushed one button near the door. The floor parted, and a round bed big enough to hold five people comfortably rose into where empty space had been moments before. As the bed rotated slowly, Big Jam pushed another button. The largest flat-screen TV I'd ever seen dropped from the ceiling, like the telescreens at church that displayed hymn lyrics, but with a different operative intent, at perfect viewing height.

"Big Jam loves his boudoir," Big Jam intoned. "Big Jam loves to get down in his boudoir."

In addition to loving his boudoir, Big Jam was evidently one of those people who loved to talk about themselves in the third person. I found it extremely annoying. But, hey, I was watching this TV show voluntarily, so I shouldn't complain. In fact, I was watching it with Alex in the upstairs den, with a bowl of popcorn and a pitcher of iced tea between us.

The camera came in close on Troy Winston, host of *In and Out*. The show took viewers inside the mansions of the biggest and hottest stars of music, screen, and fashion, and then went out with that star for a night on the town at their favorite restaurant and club.

That day's edition of *In and Out* featured the aforementioned Big Jam, renowned hip-hop artist, record label chief, clothing designer, and restaurateur. Big Jam, as Troy had breathlessly filled us in, had shot out of the slums of Gary, Indiana, to become one of the biggest stars of the new century. Overcoming a brutal childhood and a prison stint for armed robbery, he parlayed his hip-hop talents into an empire that was still growing. At the moment, he wore a gray tailored Armani suit with no shirt, an assortment of gold chains around his neck, and a belt with a large BJ diamond belt buckle. His feet were bare, his head shaved. He looked younger than his purported age of thirty-five.

"Hot, or not?" Alex asked me as she nibbled on some popcorn.

"He's kind of *old*," I pointed out.

"I bet he's intense. I'd do him. You?"

I shrugged uncomfortably and reached for some popcorn.

Alex cocked her head, studying me. "You don't like to talk about sex?"

Sheesh. Would she just move *on*, already?

"It's okay," I managed to reply.

Her eyes lit up. "Wait. You can't possibly be . . . You really are a *virgin*!"

My face reddened. "You don't have to say it like it's a disease."

She nudged me playfully. "This is like finding some fossil that's never been seen before. A hot-blooded, cute American girl who has never—"

I bonked her with a throw pillow.

"It's sweet, really," she insisted through her laughter. "I don't know anyone who's a virgin. Well, actually I do, now. You. How . . . how quaint."

My face burned, as much from the fact that I'd just come close to lying outright to my best friend in Los Angeles as from Alex's bemused reaction. I felt ashamed. Here was Alex, a girl with a real past, who had every reason to lie about it or minimize it to me, but never did. Here I was, the new girl, who could just as easily have told the truth that she'd had sex exactly once in her life, the night before she came to California, with a guy who had been her boyfriend for months, but was wondering in the aftermath if he was truly the right guy for her.

There was no reason for me to hide the truth, except that the truth didn't exactly square with the image I wanted to have of myself. Or the image I wanted Alex to have of me.

Alex seemed on the verge of saying something else when the TV caught her eye again. Big Jam had moved to his wine cellar, the camera panning across five thousand bottles of fine wine from around the world, plus casks of aging single malt Scotch, which he planned to market under the Big Jam label.

Alex slumped against the couch as the camera moved into a walk-in refrigerator full of expensive French champagne.

"Taittinger." She sighed. "Taittinger is the best. I used to love Taittinger."

I remembered that Kent Stevens had served the same champagne. It had to be excellent. This had to suck for her. Coming out of rehab, to see all that alcohol. I took the remote and changed the channel at random. We ended up on *SpongeBob*.

She whirled at me. "What are you doing?"

"I'm . . . I'm protecting you," I told her hesitantly. "I can't imagine what it's like to be looking at all those bottles after—after the problems that you had."

"Turn it back," she said stonily.

"Why?"

"Just turn it back, dammit. Do I need a reason?"

I froze. Did she want me to go back because she was enjoying the temptation of looking at booze? Or did she see this segment as some kind of test of character? Or was it something else that I didn't understand or couldn't understand?

I pushed channel return. We came back to *In and Out*. Fortunately, they had cut to a commercial for an acne scrub.

"Sorry," Alex mumbled. "I didn't mean to be that harsh."

"What just happened?"

She ran her fingers through her thick hair. "The world goes on, you know? Whether I stay sober or not. People are going to drink, do drugs, party—even people I know. Actually, make that *especially* people I know. I can't shut the world out. All I can do is take it one day at a time and learn to deal."

I understood, I thought. On the other hand, I'm not sure that if I was Alex, I'd want to be voluntarily spending time looking at an amazing wine cellar. Which is exactly what I told her.

"I pick my spots." She lifted a glass of iced tea and regarded it sadly. "Sometimes, like with my old friends, I'll be cautious. Like, not going to the overlook in Pacific Palisades. I know what they like to do there. It's what I used to like to do there. But a TV show? Like this one? I have to learn how to handle it. What am I going to do when I'm on the freeway and I see a billboard for beer? Close my eyes?"

I nodded. "Got it."

"I knew there was a reason I liked you." Her smile was genuinely grateful.

In and Out came back on; Big Jam was in his art gallery. His collection came from all over the world, from everyplace he had traveled. It made me think that private art galleries must be as much a sign of being rich and famous in Los Angeles as pickup trucks were a sign of being an average Minnesotan. Big Jam walked through his gallery, pointing out his favorite sculptures. This one from Tokyo. This one from Havana. This one from Peru. Like that. Then his face lit up as he spotted someone or something out of camera range.

"Baby girl!"

The camera zeroed in on a petite young black woman about my age in the entryway to the gallery. She wore black trousers and a white tank top. Her arms were folded, and dreadlocks framed her beautiful face. And I realized—

"Oh my God! I know her. That's Mia!"

"Mia who?"

"This girl I know from church." As *In and Out* showed a brief and none-too-warm conversation between Big Jam and Mia, who was apparently his daughter, I shared the condensed version of how I had met Mia, right down to how I was sad that we hadn't exchanged phone numbers. "And she's Big Jam's *daughter?*"

Alex laughed. "Well, now you can find her. If you can get past Big Jam's bodyguards."

I just shook my head. "This is so weird. She was church shopping. And she said she didn't feel like she ever fit in. I think you'd like her."

"Maybe," Alex replied. "But if she's church shopping?"

"What?"

"Let me repeat that I'm not. Not now, not ever."

An hour later, Alex had gone home, and I had finished a brief text conversation with my friend Shelby back in Minnesota. She reported that life was boring without me there, but as I knew, it was reasonably boring in Mankato even with me there. I asked her to come visit; I told her that she was welcome anytime. Even after the snacks with Alex, I was still hungry, so I went down to the kitchen to see what was in the fridge. I found my mom at the kitchen table, dressed in her favorite maroon sweats, with piles of papers on all sides of her and a yellow legal pad in front of her. I knew what that meant. She always wrote the first drafts of her sermons on legal pads.

Oops. Her legal pad was blank. Which meant either that

she was just starting, or that she was having a hard time. Or both.

"Hey, sweetie," she greeted me.

"Hey." I opened the fridge. "Writer's block?"

"You want to take a crack at this?" She pushed the legal pad in my direction and put down her blue Bic pen. "Because I'm not making a whole lot of progress here."

"Have you talked to Dad?" I took an apple from the fridge. I'd seen my mom stuck before. Sometimes my father had some good suggestions.

"I don't want to bother him," she confessed. "He's in his office polishing his manuscript. Kent Stevens wants it perfect before he takes it to the studios, on the off chance that someone might actually want to read the whole thing. He's so excited, your father. This is like a dream come true."

I chomped on my apple and surveyed all the piles on the table. One was obviously financial. Another was correspondence. Another looked like government reports of some kind. There was another that was just checks to the Church of Beverly Hills. Big checks. I saw one for fifty thousand dollars. Kent Stevens had written it.

"Is this a dream come true for you?"

My mom rubbed her eyes with the knuckles of each hand. "I look at my family. Everyone is so happy. Chad loves his swimming. Gemma loves her new friends and that she's getting to be on TV. Your father? Look at him. He's practically *glowing*. You seem to be doing fine. So yes. I'd say it's a dream come true."

"What about *you*?" I asked. "Are you having fun?"

She smiled mirthlessly. "Nothing gets past you."

"Not much," I agreed, sliding into the chair across from her. "So?"

She straightened a pile of papers that didn't need straightening. "I'm ambivalent. On the one hand, I have a tremendous amount of influence on people who have a lot of influence on other people's lives. I'm on vacation from radio now, but if I get a national show? That's a once-in-a-lifetime opportunity. How can that not be good?"

"But?" I prompted her.

"But I'm so tired and stressed that I can't write a decent sermon. Working until nine at night six days a week. We have so much less family time."

"Sounds like someone needs a hug." I heard my father's voice as he came bouncing into the kitchen in a pair of khaki shorts and a golf shirt. He bent down and hugged my mom from behind, planting a kiss on the top of her head. "How goes it, love?"

My mom shook her head. "Maybe the real writer in the family should take a crack at my sermon. Because the fake writer in the family isn't having very much luck."

My dad pulled up a chair facing backward. "Maybe you could talk about how God gave a well-deserved break to your long-struggling husband, by having his new novel optioned for the movies."

"Not so sure God had anything to do with that, Charlie," my mother opined.

I agreed.

My father smacked his chest. "Wounded! Wounded by my own wife and daughter. How tragic!"

I couldn't help smiling. I couldn't remember ever seeing him this happy.

My mom's BlackBerry sounded; she'd left it on the table. She sighed again—her third sigh in the past ten minutes. "Some church crisis," she guessed.

She was wrong. It was a Minnesota number on her caller ID. "Donna Thiessen," she announced, sounding surprised and happy. Donna was the longtime president of our church in Mankato, and a family friend.

"Put her on speaker so we can all say hi," my dad suggested.

A moment later, Donna's familiar flat tones filled the kitchen. I had a moment of homesickness when she said how much everyone missed us.

"I'm gonna get right to the point," she went on. "We're having some problems with your replacement, Marsha. That fellow we brought in from Duluth? Peter Hayes? A lot of people aren't warming to him."

"I'm sure he'll work out," my mom responded diplomatically. "Sometimes it takes a while."

"And sometimes if the fit isn't good at the beginning, all you end up waiting for is blisters the size of the Metrodome," Donna observed.

"I wish there was something I could do for you." My mom was sympathetic.

"Oh, but there is." Donna's voice was grave, and she let the silence build the tension. "You, Charlie, and the kids? You can come on home. The board asked me to make this call. We *need* you, Marsha. Your job is waiting for you. All you have to do is say yes."

Chapter Fourteen

The morning after the phone call from Mankato—my mother had told Donna that she was flattered but that she'd made a commitment here, and then retired to the outside deck by herself, refusing my dad's offer of company—was when the church youth group was supposed to go to the Sepulveda Basin park in the San Fernando Valley and volunteer at the weekly outdoor soup kitchen.

Ha.

The day dawned with a rare June downpour of nearly biblical proportions. I'd been warned about the so-called June Gloom of Southern California, which was when the marine layer from the ocean collided with the hot inland temperatures to create an impenetrable blanket of fog. But rain so intense that television networks kept cutting to their meteorologists for "storm watch" updates? During which the TV helicopters were grounded, and crews showed streets utterly inundated? Obviously, this didn't happen very often.

Just as obviously, the outdoor soup kitchen in the 818 was completely washed out. Gemma woke up with a stomach bug and would have had to stay home anyway, so she wasn't all that upset, even though she'd been looking forward to hanging with her new church friends. As for my mom, she hated to see a teen volunteer force go to waste, so she worked the phones for an hour after her morning coffee, looking for some other endeavor that would allow us to do good works of which she could approve.

As someone from the pediatrics department at the UCLA hospital put her on hold, I mouthed, "Please make sure it's *inside*."

UCLA didn't want us—some legal thing about our being underage. That seemed ironic, because most of the kids I'd met in Beverly Hills had fake IDs. You could find a way to *drink* underage; you just couldn't find a way to do *charity* underage.

As my mother made calls, I went upstairs to my room to play my new guitar and muck around on my computer. I had no idea whether Sean was working that day, but we hadn't really checked in since he'd texted me about his tentative itinerary. I'd given it a lot of thought. I was not opposed to a boyfriend from Minnesota coming here. I just wanted to make sure that the boyfriend who was coming was really my boyfriend. Maybe I wouldn't have scrutinized our relationship so much if we were both still in Mankato, but now things were long-distance. Long-distance? I wanted a boyfriend—I needed a boyfriend—who would share what was in his heart with me, the same way I would share my heart with him.

As the rain beat against the hummingbird feeder and my window, I texted Sean to see what was going on. It turned out he was home; he had the morning off. Three minutes later, we were at our respective laptops, webcams activated, talking to each other on Skype.

My video came up first, then his, which meant he got a look at me before I could see him. I was wearing a black men's undershirt and a pair of gray shorts. Nothing special. But Sean still exclaimed when he saw me.

"Nat? Wow! What did you do to your *hair?*"

Whoa. That's right. He hadn't seen me on Skype since I'd gone with Alex to Agua. Well, now I'd have to talk about it.

His video popped up on my screen. He wore a green tennis shirt and looked exactly the same as he had when I saw him last.

"I went with a friend to a spa here," I explained. "They're called extensions. You like?"

"Yeah, I like, I guess. But it doesn't look like you. I just have to get used to it. How much did it cost?" He leaned back in his desk chair and laced his fingers behind his head.

"I don't know," I said honestly.

"What do you mean you don't know?" he said challengingly.

"They were a present. From the girl who took me to the spa. So it didn't cost me anything."

"It had to cost someone something," he went on. Was I wrong, or was there a distinct note of derision in his voice? "Someone had to pay for it. Who's the new friend?"

Crap. I really did not want to get into the subject of Alex

Samuels if he was going to be hostile. On the other hand, I told myself that I wanted emotional honesty from Sean; I'd better start by being emotionally honest myself.

"Her name is Alexis—Alex—Samuels. She's a neighbor of ours. Sean?"

"Yeah?"

"She has a past," I said. "She used to be a party girl, but now she's changed."

To my surprise, he smiled. "Ah. You met her at church. Is your mother working her usual magic?"

I was blunt. "Alex doesn't go to church."

Sean raised his eyebrows. "Ah. Not your church."

"Not any church. None at all. That's her choice."

"You're trying to change her mind, of course," he prompted me.

"Nope. Like I said, that's her choice." I folded my arms defiantly. Then my voice softened. "How do you feel about that?"

He shrugged. "Okay, I guess."

"Come on, you have to feel more than that."

He shook his head. "Nope. It doesn't matter to me one way or the other, really. She's your friend, not mine."

I could sense it. A paramecium could sense it. He was shutting down on the topic. I pushed a little. "It's okay, you know, if you're worried, or angry. I won't melt."

He shrugged again. "I'm okay. It's your life, it's your friend. Let's change the subject, okay? Did you check with your parents yet about those dates? For when I can come to Los Angeles?"

My stomach lurched a little. "No. Not yet. My mom's been kinda crazed."

"Well, do it soon. Because it's okay on my end. And I can't wait to see you."

"I will," I told him, which was the truth. Then I took a deep breath. Maybe this was the time to talk to Sean about my worries about us, about how hesitant I was feeling about him. About how this conversation wasn't helping.

Just then, though, Sean got a text from his boss at the mall. There'd been some sort of oil spill in the parking lot, and he was being summoned to work immediately.

"Let me know when you talk to your folks," he said quickly. "Gotta go. Love you."

Thus endeth the conversation. It seemed like a good time to take another look at my song "The Shape I'm In." I opened my notebook.

The sun sets bright, it rises dim,
That's the measure of the shape I'm in.
The ice it warms me, the heat it chills,
That's the measure of the games and the thrills.
The sun sets bright, it rises dim,
That's the measure of the shape I'm in.

Sleep wears me out, life makes me sleep,
That's the measure when I try to go deep.
The sun sets bright, it rises dim,
That's the measure of the shape I'm in.

I added a few lines that I thought made sense, considering the weather.

The rain dries me out, the sun soaks my soul.
If the drummer played faster, it could be rock 'n'
roll.
No rainbow coming, more clouds moving in,
That's the measure of the shape I'm in.

Decent. I was about to try another verse, but my mom texted me to come to the kitchen. She'd found a volunteer project for our youth group.

The Church of Beverly Hills was a cosponsor of the largest interfaith homeless shelter in the county, located near Pershing Square downtown. It was called the Tom Bradley Shelter, after a former mayor of Los Angeles, and it served the needs of hundreds of homeless people every day.

When I went back downstairs, it turned out that my mother had just talked with the director, LaVonne Williams. I learned later that LaVonne had been homeless herself, but with the assistance of the staff at this very shelter, she'd worked up to master's degrees in both administration and counseling. When my mom told LaVonne that she had fifty kids from several congregations ready to roll up their sleeves and go to work, LaVonne had literally shouted, "Praise the Lord!"

Which is how it came to be that two hours later, I was riding in a church minivan—fortunately, not the limousine van, but a regular one—downtown, past the Staples Center and the public library, toward a sprawling warehouse of a building located a block from Pershing Square, a park better known for its drug trade than for its flora and fauna.

We navigated the sodden streets, rain pounding at the van

windows. I was in the backseat between Sandra and a girl named Courtney, who had a blunt blond bob and California-tanned skin. Everyone was wearing variations of jeans, T-shirts, and hoodies. I couldn't help noticing the logo on Courtney's hoodie. D&G. It had to have cost a fortune.

Meanwhile, I was being chatted up by a guy in front of me named Fitz, which was short for Fitzgerald. He was cute enough in a retro hippie kind of way, with a wispy goatee, a blond ponytail, and a tie-dyed T-shirt. He said he attended a private school called Harvard-Westlake, where he was on their math team, and also played Ultimate Frisbee. He had an endless supply of make-you-groan jokes, most of them directed at me. Sandra nudged me and gave me that raised-eyebrow "he likes you" look. I just couldn't see him like that. Between texts from Sean about the overturned tanker truck near the mall and daydreams about Brett, I had already overloaded the "guy" space in my brain.

As Fitz cracked more jokes, my mind drifted to Brett. We'd made our date. Friday night, a week from that night. He didn't want to say where. "Let me surprise you," he'd said. "You seem like a girl who likes surprises."

I wrote back to say that I'd keep my busy social schedule open for Friday, and that yes, I was a girl who enjoyed surprises. Of course, I can't think of a single time a guy in Minnesota surprised me, even with a dating destination. This could well be because in Mankato and the surrounding hamlets, there was a very limited number of destinations from which to choose.

Brett had texted that even though Temple Emanuel was supposed to be sending a group of kids to work at the soup kitchen, he couldn't be there, since he'd be shooting a segment of *Working Stiff*. Could I please ladle some soup on his behalf? I thought that was sweet. But then, looking back, I realize I was in that infatuation stage, when everything the guy says seems sweet or funny or really deep. Don't try to tell me you haven't been there, too.

The van made a left turn into a parking lot and stopped at a guard gate, where the security people let us pass. The shelter had been built in an out-of-use warehouse, and the line of homeless and hungry people waiting to use its various services stretched from the door all the way to the street. We passed hundreds of people of all races, colors, and ages, tucked under a Spartan sheet metal and framework canopy that only semi-shielded them from the rain. When the wind blew, they got drenched.

I saw a tan Asian mother in a housedress, holding the hands of two toddlers. An elderly black man with a hat fashioned out of aluminum foil. Four huge Latino guys in matching T-shirts and black shorts. A cluster of kids our age who had that raggedy look of having lived out-of-doors for too long a time. More people like that. My heart turned over.

"It shouldn't be like this," Sandra murmured, staring out the window. "Not in America."

Courtney nodded. "And *definitely* not in L.A." She tapped a finger against the glass. "Look at those two cute little girls. They don't even have jackets!"

The snippy thought that came to mind was *You could have bought decent clothes for those kids instead of your D&G hoodie.*

I surveyed the line again as it slowly snaked forward. To my surprise, I saw some well-dressed people, who didn't look like they belonged there at all. Yet they were here in the pouring rain for the free lunch that started at eleven o'clock. Maybe they even wanted one of the beds, where they could spend the night for free.

The surprise must have registered on my face.

"The economy," Fitz said knowledgably, stroking his wispy goatee. "Since the downturn, with the state running out of money, shelters are, like, overrun."

"There really aren't jobs for these people?"

Fitz shook his head sadly. I was actually a little bit shocked. In the shelter back home where I did volunteer work one night a month in the winter, most of our "guests" were on the verge of certifiable and utterly unable to work. Twice I'd had to call someone from the hospital psych unit.

With Mr. Bienvenu at the wheel—I found it hard to call him by his first name, as he asked us to—our van rolled on, joining several other vans and buses parked by the side of the building. Each was from a different house of worship. I saw the white one from Brett's temple right away and felt a moment's disappointment that he wouldn't be here. There were others— from a Roman Catholic church in Alhambra, a mosque in Carson, and a Lutheran church in Hancock Park.

We all piled out, dashing inside through the downpour. We were led into a nondescript multipurpose room filled with rows of cheap metal folding chairs, where we joined the other volunteers. As soon as everyone was seated, we got the quickest orientation in history from LaVonne Williams herself. She was tall and imposing. When her deep, resonant voice rang out, she reminded me of the famous poet Maya Angelou.

She wandered down the center aisle as she spoke. Most of

us would be serving lunch. Some of us would be doing intake for people who needed social or medical services. Some of us would be doing a deep clean in the dormitories. Some of us would be working in the free clothing area, and some would be making phone calls, trying to raise additional funds for the shelter.

LaVonne gestured to several staff members who had entered with signs detailing the assignments. "Go to the station that most interests you, but fair warning: if the stations aren't balanced, staff will move you around." She paused to make sure there were no questions. "We appreciate your help so much. Thanks for being you."

The volunteers applauded politely and the orientation broke up. Sandra and Courtney asked me if I wanted to go sort clothes, but I was more interested in seeing what life in the shelter was like. I decided to volunteer for the cleaning crew and made my way across the room to the lady holding the sign for it. When I reached her, I felt a tap on my back.

Brett Goldstein.

He was wearing black jeans and a black T-shirt and was more or less soaked. In fact, he was mopping his wet hair with a dark towel as he grinned at me. Do I even need to tell you how surprised and happy I was to see him?

"Come here often?" he asked nonchalantly.

"You said you had a shoot!"

He put his arms out to me. "Canceled due to rain," he explained, and gave me a quick damp hug. "We were supposed to be on location at the La Brea Tar Pits."

"The *what* pits?"

"Los Angeles natural wonder. I'll take you sometime. Anyway, I called a bud, who told me all the volunteers had ended up here, and here I am."

"There you are," I echoed, the same idiotic smile of joy still plastered to my face. "I'm glad you're here."

"So am I. And Natalie?"

"Yeah?"

"This does not qualify as our first date."

We were a small group. Cleaning crew was hardly anyone else's first choice. For the next two hours, we scrubbed bathrooms. Literally. We were given two buckets full of ammonia water, two mops, two scrub brushes, and two rolls of paper towels and told to make the main bathrooms spotless. Each bathroom serviced one of the three dormitories. Each dorm had nearly a hundred beds, which meant the bathrooms were huge. The women's bathroom, for example, had ten shower stalls, sinks, and toilets, plus changing areas. Cleaning them was no simple matter, but it felt great to be working with Brett. He was even more disciplined than I was, not taking a break until he'd worked his way through all the shower stalls and I'd finished the sinks and changing areas. We'd agreed to tackle the toilets together, leaving the mirrors and the floor for last.

I was just doing the last of the sinks when my cell rang. I checked caller ID: it was Alex. As I moved to answer it, I heard Brett's cell ring. His ringtone was a song by one of my favorite bands, the Shins.

"Hey, Alex!" I looked for someplace to sit. There were some benches by the sinks, and I headed for one. Meanwhile,

Brett indicated that because of the echo, he'd take his call outside. I waved to say I understood.

"Hey. What are you doing on this glorious day?" Alex asked.

"Well, I'm with Brett, and I stink," I replied, using my forearm to wipe sweaty hair from my forehead. I told her about my church volunteer project and how I'd run into and was working with Brett.

She laughed. "His cell just rang, right?"

"How did you know?" I rubbed at a knot on my left shoulder. Repetitive motion will do that to you.

"Because I'm at Brooke's, and we decided we're having a party tonight, and I told her that I would call you, and she said she would call Brett, and she's sitting in the hot tub—it's great in the rain!— with me right now, on the phone with him. Say hi, Brooke!"

I heard a muffled "Hi, Brooke!"

"So we're having this party, and we're inviting you and Brett and a bunch of other people, and I wanted to know if you would come." Alex laughed again. "I have a feeling Brett will be there."

I wasn't sure exactly what to say. First, I wasn't sure if I could go, or even if I would be allowed to go. My mother had a big fund-raiser dinner that night, and I didn't know if my dad had plans. If Gemma was sick, someone would have to stay home with her and Chad. Second, I wasn't sure that being at a party was the smartest thing for Alex. Parties meant partying, after all, and I thought that if Brooke was in charge, the main drink would more likely be Long Island Iced Tea, which has like a zillion different kinds of alcohol in it, than Lipton. Of course, if this was going to be a Brooke-type party and Alex was definitely going to attend, it would probably be a good idea for me to be there, too. Then again, my parents knew enough about Hollywood kids by now that even the Alex factor might not be enough for them to let me attend. Too much temptation. Too much Long Island Iced Tea.

Then there was the at-a-party-with-Brett factor. *That* I liked. Sure, Skye could well be there. In fact, she'd probably be there. But I took Brett at his word. If something serious came up with someone else, then Brett-and-Skye wasn't a big impediment. In fact, it wasn't an impediment at all. If he was stretching the truth on that issue, I'd find out sooner rather than later, which was a good thing.

I hoped my dad would want to stay home that night with Gemma and Chad. Since his novel had been optioned, he'd been obsessed with writing, which meant my butt was probably covered.

Which was why I said, "I'd love to come."

Chapter Fifteen

"Your mother just called," my dad announced as he let me in the front door. Somehow, I'd misplaced my house key. Probably it was in one of the shower stalls at the downtown shelter. Maybe I'd lost it when Brett offered to rub my sore neck. I could still feel his hands on me, gently kneading my muscles.

"Earth to Natalie?" My father waved a hand in front of my face.

"Sorry, Dad. What?"

I kicked out of my sodden running shoes. I'd had to wade through a puddle to reboard the bus. Though the rain had eased in the afternoon, it picked up again after Mr. Bienvenu had dropped us all back at the church. From there, because of street closures and nearly impossible traffic, it had taken me an hour to get to Ricardo's mansion. I didn't pull the Saturn through the gate until nearly six.

"Instead of drinks at the Beverly Hills Hotel, they took her downtown. Kent Stevens wants her on the board of some city agency; he was going to introduce her to the mayor."

My dad had thoughtfully put down some towels in the foyer so wet feet wouldn't destroy the flooring. I took off my white socks—they were as soaked as my sneakers—and wiped my bare feet on a gray towel as I sniffed the air, which smelled of tomato and garlic.

"Spaghetti sauce?" I asked hopefully. My dad was a more-than-decent cook.

Dad gave a mock bow. "Hey. I live to serve."

"Mom's going from the meeting to the donors' dinner?" I asked.

"Straightaway. Do not pass Go, do not collect two hundred dollars."

"Are you meeting her there?" I asked. Not that I wanted him to. I wanted him in all night so I could go to Brooke's party.

"It's pretty clear that I wasn't invited," Dad reported, to my relief. "I guess your mother could have pressed the point, but . . . well, it's different here from Minnesota."

I understood. In Mankato, whenever my mom had any kind of a function that involved food, whether it was a board meeting or the annual Mankato Little League awards dinner, where she'd deliver the invocation, my father was asked to be there, too. Here in Los Angeles? It was different. Very different.

I balled up the used towel. "Well, maybe after she's been here for a while." I wanted to offer some support, even though on the inside I was singing. Yes, feel free to call me a hypocrite.

He gave a little laugh. "Maybe. Anyway, it worked out for

the best tonight. I would have had to stay home with your sister anyway."

"Then you should be grateful," I told him.

"A little," he admitted. "I'd feel better if I weren't worried about Mom."

I was glad he said it. Because I was worried, too. She seemed so stressed. Back in Minnesota, she'd worked hard. It hadn't been unusual for her to do something church-related every day of the week, even though her nominal day off was Monday. But the new job was huge. Her BlackBerry was always sounding. She checked it more often than a politician, and I wondered if that was what she felt like—a newly elected politician—constantly taking the pulse of her constituency, constantly checking her poll numbers, constantly worried that the honeymoon of the first weeks in office would give way to the reality of marriage.

There were so many people watching her, counting on her, wanting her time. "She's so busy," I mused. "She's never been good at saying no when someone needs her."

"Yeah," Dad agreed. "Hey, don't you worry, sweetie. I'll talk to your mom. But now I need to get back to my sauce."

"Gemma's ready to eat pasta?"

"Gemma's ready to eat nothing. She's on tea and toast and has a temp of a hundred and one."

"Is she feeling any better?"

My dad cocked his head at my feet. "Marginally. You should put your slippers on. I believe I saw them in the front hall closet."

"I'm actually going to shower," I said. "What about Chad? Did he swim today?"

"I think he has a touch of whatever Gemma has, too. He's in his room playing some addictive video game. His practice was canceled."

I went upstairs, took the world's quickest shower, pulled on some jeans and a cozy sweater, then went back down to the kitchen. Dad was stirring his sauce with a wooden spoon, and fusilli pasta was draining in a colander. The table was already set for us; he motioned me to it.

"This looks fab, Dad," I said when I sat down.

He took a cucumber-and-dill salad he'd made earlier from the fridge, and put the rest of the food on the table. "Today the Shelton house, tomorrow *Top Chef*." He slid into the seat across from me and nodded at me to say grace.

One of our family traditions was that grace could not be rote. It had to be original and in the moment. I thought about my day. The image of that huge line of people waiting for food, clothing, and shelter at the homeless shelter flashed brightly in my mind. Then Brett flashed through my mind. And the party I wanted to go to, and . . .

I mentally chided myself and headed back to the thoughts of the shelter.

"God," I began, "we thank you for the good things in our life, for our good luck and fortune, and for life itself. May we enjoy this meal while remembering your gifts and remember always to bring your gifts to others, for here on earth your work truly is our own. Bless this table and this home in Jesus's name. Amen."

My father looked at me with something approaching awe. "That was inspiring, Natalie. Really."

I felt embarrassed. All it was, was heartfelt.

"Thank you."

"I hope you have the chance to sit at a table sometime with your eldest daughter and hear her offer grace like that."

Okay. I admit it. I choked up a little at those words. We ate in silence for a few minutes. His fusilli was, as always, incredible. I saw that my dad was chewing with gusto. I took the moment to ask if I could go to the party.

Dad wiped his mouth with a white paper napkin. "Who's giving it?"

"A friend of Alex's, named Brooke. It's at her place."

"Will her parents be home?"

"Yep," I replied.

Okay, you may note here that I had no idea whether Brooke's parents would in fact be home. I'm a teenager, not a saint.

My dad nodded. "Your cell is charged?"

"Definitely."

"You know my cell by heart? And the landline number here? Just in case you lose your cell?"

That was *so* my father. Thinking ahead, figuring out what to do in a situation that wouldn't be a problem until it became a problem.

Anyway, he'd nailed me. There was indeed a landline at the mansion, presumably for emergencies when film crews rented it out. I had the number programmed in my cell. But by heart? Ha.

"I know your number. I'll write down the landline," I promised.

"Good." He smiled. "Then go. Have fun. And use—"

"Good judgment," I said with him. My mom and he had been telling me that forever, based on the theory that if something is important to you, then you shouldn't shut up about it.

"What time can I expect you home?"

"I don't know. No later than midnight, I guess." Twelve had been my consistent curfew in Mankato. Since the town basically rolled up at eleven, staying out till midnight was no great shakes. "Will that work?"

"Hey, you're about to go into your senior year of high school, and you're in Los Angeles." He slurped up some more spaghetti and grinned at me. "Make it one."

"Are you ready to rock and roll? I said, are you ready, ready, ready to rock and roll?"

"Yeah!" The crowd of two or three hundred high school kids who'd been drinking, dancing, swimming, and cavorting in the party space—there was no other way to describe it— behind Brooke Summers's ivy-covered mansion shouted as one as the lead singer from the Sex Puppets egged them on with a raised fist. Evidently, Brooke was kinda-sorta dating the drummer, which was how she had been able to get them for a last-minute gig.

"I can't hear you!"

"Yeah!" the crowd cheered again.

"I can't hear you!"

This time, the roar from the crowd was deafening, and the band's guitarist decided that he could start the next song. The band started to wail, and all thoughts of conversation were swept up in their infectious, eighties-influenced power pop.

As people all around me started to dance, I stared up at the crystalline moonlit sky. It had turned out to be a beautiful night. As quickly as the rain clouds had moved in before dawn, they'd moved out just before sunset, leaving the city glistening and spotlessly clean. The air, usually polluted by millions of car-commute miles, had been rubbed, scrubbed, and rescrubbed by the downpour. The sunset had been magnificent as the sun dropping behind the Pacific lit the city in hues of blue, purple, and pink that artists could only ever dream about.

"Want to dance?" Alex's voice took me out of my reverie.

"What?"

"Come on!"

She took my hand and led me into the seething mass of humanity in front of the stage that had been erected at the south end of the Summers's double tennis court.

Let me say that back in Mankato, dancing with my girlfriends was no big deal, and we had lots of fun at parties. But they were nothing like this.

In Mankato, you park your own car and walk in the front door. You say hello to the parents of whoever is giving the party, and you go into the basement, or you go out back.

Here, Brooke had valet parking for her guests. The Latino valet snickered when he took my Saturn. No wonder, since the car in front of me was an Aston Martin, and the one behind me a Jaguar. But at least I didn't have to worry about where to put my car. There was a line of golf carts—also driven by uniformed Latino guys—to shuttle guests from the gate to the house, so I climbed onto the backseat of one of them, and away I went.

Alex had told me that Brooke's family was only partly a showbiz family. Her mother was a famous independent-film producer. One of her films, *Mocking Bird Lane*—about a boy named Lane who thought he could fly and, magically, just once, did fly—had been nominated for a Golden Globe. Brooke's mother could finance her movies because Brooke's father was the sole owner of a construction business that didn't just build houses. He built freeways, factories, and high-rise office buildings. The *L.A. Times* had recently reported that he'd received a multibillion-dollar contract to renovate the entire port of Long Beach, a project expected to take five years.

Constructing all that good stuff meant he had ample funds to invest in his own dwelling. Brooke's house—I kid you not—looked from the front like the White House, only with a nicer porch. But I never got inside, since the golf cart took me around back, where the party was under way.

Alex had asked me to text her on my arrival. I did, and she was waiting for me at the drop-off point. She wore a pale pink minidress with brown high-heeled booties and greeted me with a huge hug. "You look hot!"

I'd made an effort to do my hair and makeup and put on a short black skirt and a white tank top. I didn't think I looked fantastic, but I didn't look out of place, either, unless you knew that my outfit was from Target. I took in the guys and girls arriving, already in full party mode, many with beers in hand. Rock and roll blared from speakers somewhere below us, and we could hear the whoops and screams of kids apparently jumping into a pool, as yet unseen.

Alex took me on a tour of the back, and at least I didn't

look like a bobble-head doll, searching for Brett. He'd told me before we left the shelter that he was having Saturday night dinner with his parents and brother and wouldn't be able to come to the party until ten-thirty at the earliest. That was fine with me. It gave me more time to start feeling less out of place.

The backyard—and the party—was on three tiers. The top tier was landscaped, with dozens of tables and chairs for hanging out, plus chaise lounges and swings. The main bars and buffet stations were up here. There was one station for Japanese, another for Mexican, and yet another for vegetarian alternatives. I saw kids lined up at the bars and saw that Coke, juice, and iced tea were not the only things being served. I raised my eyebrows questioningly at Alex.

"Not to worry," she told me. "That's why we're going down below."

"I'm with you," I assured her.

"I know. That's why I feel great."

We went down a long, broad white set of marble steps to the second level, the pool level. Or I should say, pools level. The main pool was shaped like a teardrop. Another was rectangular, with waterslides and a high dive, and there were three hot tubs. Each featured dozens of kids in various stages of undress, and a cannonball contest was under way at the high dive. Two huge guys turned and lowered their surfer jams, mooning the crowd.

"These are your future classmates," Alex quipped as they sent up huge splashes of water.

"Yeah. And one day their vote will count just as much as yours and mine."

Alex laughed and linked her arm through mine. I could feel curious eyes on me as she led me around the teardrop pool and toward yet another long staircase. Who's the girl with Alex? Never saw *her* before.

Finally, we were on the lower level, where the twin tennis courts had been transformed into music-and-dance central. In addition to the raised stage for the Sex Puppets, professional lighting towers had been erected, so the whole thing approximated a nightclub experience. Not that I'd ever been to a nightclub. But I'd seen them on TV.

That was how it came to be that Alex and I were dancing.

"Loosen up!" She spun and swung her ass at me sexily, then pushed her hands overhead, up toward the moon.

Oh. What the heck.

I danced like Alex was dancing. I didn't do as well as she did, but I tried. And I liked it. It was fun. Really fun. As I danced, I felt a pair of hands take hold of my waist and dance with me from behind. I swiveled to tell Mr. Wandering Hands to shove off. Then I saw who it was and grinned.

For the second time that day, Brett Goldstein had surprised me.

Chapter Sixteen

The first thing I did was take a surreptitious look around, to
see if Brett was with Skye. Nope. No Skye. Then we danced,
the three of us, for so many songs I lost track. Sometimes it
was Brett and me, with Alex egging us on. Sometimes it was
Brett and Alex, with me dancing around them like a siren.
Sometimes it was Alex and me, Brett to one side, all of us
rocking out to the Sex Puppets. The music got faster and
faster, till they thrashed through their last song like the Drop-
kick Murphys on a caffeine overdose.

After the final song, the crowd whooped. The lead singer
announced a thirty-minute break, and Alex told us she was
going to find a bathroom in one of the cabanas. That left Brett
and me alone, which was not necessarily a bad thing. It got
even better when Pinhead Gunpowder came on the sound system with their version of "Big Yellow Taxi," and Brett suggested that the two of us take a walk to yet another area of

Brooke's back forty, down a cobblestone path to a secluded gazebo and pond illuminated by burning torches, far enough away that the party noise was a dull roar.

Someone had thoughtfully put a cooler of soft drinks, beer, and champagne in the center of the gazebo. Brett went to the cooler and extracted a bottle of champagne. "You like?"

I shook my head. "Not a big drinker." Truth was I wasn't a drinker at all.

"Then let's go with fizzy water." He traded the champagne for a couple of bottles of Lauretana—which I found really sweet and considerate—and handed one to me. "Here's to new friends."

Definitely. "To new friends."

We clinked bottles and drank. And then we talked. Really talked. He asked me more about Mankato. And then he told me about Beverly Hills. Growing up where each one of your friends is richer than the next? "It's unreal."

He rubbed the cold bottle against his forehead. My heart beat faster when he did. I reached surreptitiously into my pocketbook and turned my cell to silent. If Sean was picking this moment to call me or text me, I didn't want to know right now.

"Do they get it right on TV?" I asked. "You know. Like *90210*."

"Nah," Brett scoffed, and tipped his head back for a long guzzle.

"Yeah, I figured that was all exaggerated to get people to watch."

"No, I meant in real life, it's worse," he said. "Life turns into a competition, a pretty dumb-ass competition. Like, take this party." He swept his hands back toward the tennis courts, the pool, and beyond. "How much do you think Brooke spent on it?"

I shrugged. "I have no idea. A thousand dollars?"

Brett hooted. "You have a lot to learn. Your car got parked by the valet on the way here?"

I nodded.

"That's two grand right there. I'd say the total for the night, from start to finish, including the Dangerous Angels cleaning crew to come in and repair the damage—and mind you, there will be damage—twelve thou, easy. Possibly fifteen. And this is something Brooke threw together at the last minute."

I was aghast. "Her parents just hand her the money?"

"Daddy's credit card," Brett explained. "But see now, the next time Skye or Alex gives a party? They'll need to spend *twenty* thou. Just to prove they can."

Skye. Even though Brett had explained their relationship, I still didn't really get it. I cleared my throat and went for a casual "So, I noticed Skye isn't here," adding a yawn.

The moment I did it, I knew it was stupid, but you can't take a yawn back.

He looked amused and copied my yawn. "You bored?"

"Not at all."

"Skye's doing a fashion show at the House of Blues tonight," Brett explained.

"But you came here instead."

He nodded, his eyes searching mine. I felt his look all the

180

way down to my toes. I didn't feel that way when Sean looked at me. I never had.

A change of subject was necessary.

"Did you know Alex's parents? Before the—you know."

He rubbed his chin thoughtfully and frowned.

"I did," he said.

I waited for him to go on, as I suspected he would. As my mother liked to say on the radio, sometimes the best thing to do in a conversation is shut up.

"They were great. Unlike most parents, they actually knew how to listen. They gave the best advice. Each of them, in their own way. Everyone liked Roger and Felicia. They asked us to call them that."

"It must have been a terrible day. The day of the crash." I had this vision of someone—maybe a reporter—calling Alex's house with the news, looking for a reaction, even before Alex knew about it. I don't know if that's plausible, but in the moment, it was what I thought.

Brett rested his forearms on his thighs and stared at the ground. "It really sucked."

He looked off into the night. He stared back over several years, and when he spoke again, his voice was almost inaudible. I literally had to cup my right ear to hear.

"There was this vigil that night," he recalled. "At their house. In the showbiz world, Roger and Felicia were pretty famous. Everyone wanted to pay their respects. There were police cruisers blocking the road, but people brought flowers on foot up to the gate."

"Did you bring some, too?"

He nodded. "The amazing thing is, we kids were allowed inside." His mouth twisted into a bitter smile. "It was like a club, where there's a guest list, and we were on it. When we walked up to the main house—there were probably six or seven of us; I remember Brooke, Skye, Gray, a few others—we didn't know what to do. The door was closed, and a cop stationed there said no visitors."

"What did you do?"

"Someone had their Mac, and we could get a wireless signal. So we sent Alex an email. Then we hung by the pool, waiting to see if she'd come down. She didn't. After a while, we just went home." In the moonlight, I thought I saw tears glistening in Brett's eyes. He turned and quickly brushed a forearm across them.

I thought about Alex inside, with her friends outside, too sad even to be with them. I'd been so lucky in my life. I had both my parents. My grandparents on both sides were still alive. On my mom's side, they'd retired to western North Carolina, where they played golf and bridge and participated in a community theater. On my dad's side, they ran a farm in northern Iowa, as you know. Come to think of it, I hadn't even lost an aunt or an uncle. I hadn't lost anyone.

Brett shifted back to me. "Scaring you off with my eternal heaviness?"

"Not at all."

"Because I am usually Mr. Cool," he insisted, clearly trying to lighten the mood.

I nodded. "Duly noted."

"If I went through what Alex went through? I'd probably end up dead before my ass ever got to rehab."

I looked toward the mansion, where a heavy bass line was thumping. Alex was up there, somewhere. "It has to be hard for her, don't you think?" I asked. "Being at this kind of party with all the alcohol?"

"Well, the world's not gonna change for her." His eyes searched mine again. "But you're still worried." He rose and tugged me to my feet. "Let's split up and find her."

As much as I would rather have stayed alone in the moonlight with Brett, I nodded. "Text me if you see her first?"

He grinned. "Only if you do the same for me."

We made our way up to the concert area together, where plenty of kids milled around, even though the Sex Puppets hadn't yet returned for their next set. No Alex. Then we went up the stairs to the pool area. That was where we separated. Brett said he'd cover the upper deck, and I told him I'd check around this level. "Text me no matter what." I was getting concerned. Where was she?

"Okay. But don't worry. This is a party and she knows everyone. It's normal." He put a strong hand on my cheek. "It'll be okay."

I wanted to stay calm, but I was worried. That I could see beer cans floating in the pool with seminude swimmers passing a joint didn't help.

I got more worried as I circumnavigated the pool, the diving area, and the hot tub. I'm pretty sure I saw a couple actually having sex in the hot tub, but I didn't see Alex. Then I remembered that she'd said she was going to use one of the bathrooms in the cabanas. I thought it was unlikely she'd still be there, but I spotted those cabanas off to the left. There were four or five doors; two were marked as bathrooms, and the rest were changing areas. I checked the bathrooms. They were apparently unisex, because there were two guys in the one to the left, and a guy and a girl in the one to the right. I muttered a "sorry" and backed away. At least the girl wasn't Alex.

That left the changing rooms.

The first one was empty.

In the second one—I had to bang on the locked door about a dozen times before it finally gave way—I got another shock in a day of major-league shocks when the door swung open. I found myself confronted by Gemma's friend Lisa Stevens. She had more clothes off than she had on.

"What part of a locked door don't you understand?" Her voice was positively caustic.

Now, I don't like being berated by a fifteen-year-old, particularly one standing there in a lacy bra and a matching thong. But it wasn't Lisa's put-down that made me upset. What she wanted to do inside a changing room at a high school party was her business, though I suspected that her father would pitch a first-class fit if he knew.

No. Lisa's enviable body and angry face weren't what threw me. The other person in the changing room with her was. Lisa was not alone. She was with my brother, Chad. My *thirteen*-year-old brother, Chad, whose clothes lay in a heap. He wore nothing but a pair of jeans.

My head spun. He was supposed to be sick! How had he gotten out of the house? What was he *doing*? Actually, I wasn't sure I wanted to know the answer to that one.

I pushed past Lisa into the changing room, where I saw a MacBook Pro open on a small table. My eyes were locked on my brother, who was both affecting a stance of defiance and staring down at the tile. Whether he was hoping it would open up so he could jump through, or hoping it would open up so I would disappear, I couldn't tell.

"Just because you look sixteen doesn't mean you *are* sixteen!" I yelled.

He got even more interested in the floor.

"For your information," Lisa began, "your brother and I were busy. Why don't you just leave?"

I whirled on her. "Get your clothes on and get out of here."

"No thanks, *Mom*," she snapped.

I got right in her face, my voice low and cold. "Get your clothes and get out, or I will throw you out."

"You go," Chad said softly to Lisa. "I'll catch up with you later."

"Busted by a big sister." Lisa laughed without a smidgeon of contrition in her voice. "That's a first for me. Just a sec."

With utter insouciance, she stepped toward my brother, pulled on a black skirt and a black sleeveless silk top, kicked into a pair of flip-flops, and then had the gall to check herself out in the changing-room mirror and rearrange her hair while I steamed. Finally, she closed up the MacBook, gave Chad a little kiss and me the finger, then left.

All thoughts of Alex were gone. It was just me and Chad.

"You get dressed, too," I ordered. "You're leaving."

"Don't tell Mom and Dad. Please." With Lisa gone, he was begging.

"What were you *thinking?*"

He didn't answer.

I fumed as my brother pulled on his sneakers and a Junior Olympics swim team T-shirt. "Just tell me you won't tell Mom and Dad," he repeated.

If he wasn't answering me, I sure as sugar wasn't answering him.

"Let's go."

I led the way past the pool, up to the main party level, and around to the front of Brooke's mansion. I didn't look at him as we took a chauffeured golf cart all the way down the hill to the valet stand. I didn't look at him when I gave my ticket to the valet, and I didn't look at him when we got in the Saturn.

I think he got the message that I was pissed. Still, he didn't say anything to me until we reached Sunset Boulevard and turned east toward our canyon.

"I can explain," he said weakly.

"I can explain, too." I kept my eyes on the road. I wasn't supposed to be driving with anyone else in the car, and didn't want to get stopped by the cops. "You faked being sick so that Mom and Dad wouldn't bother you. Dad thinks you're home sleeping and he doesn't want to wake you. Somehow—and I'm still trying to figure this one out—you snuck out of the house so that you could come to this party with Lisa. As for what you and she were doing—"

"We were making a video," Chad put in quickly.

Holy . . .

"You were making a *porno?*"

"Not that kind of video," he assured me. "A video about kissing. Like, an instructional video for YouTube. About how to kiss."

I stopped at the red light on Beverly Glen. "Yeah. Right. I'm not too dumb to live."

"You can see it yourself. I'll tell Lisa to email it to you."

I shot him a hot glance, then the light changed and I snapped my eyes back to the road. I was not getting in an accident over this. No way.

"Chad? I don't believe you. And if I did believe you, if you are somehow telling the truth, then if that video ever does end up on YouTube, you and Lisa are going to be very sorry. Am I understood?"

"I'll tell her to delete it," he said, though there was little contrition in his voice.

"Whatever it is," I fired back.

"It's a kissing video."

"Uh-huh."

I still didn't believe him, and I realized that he hadn't denied my account of how he'd come to attend the party.

The rest of the ride home was dead silent. In fact, neither of us talked until I pulled through the electric gate and started up our own driveway.

"I won't do it again," Chad promised. "I swear it. Just don't tell Mom and Dad."

"Oh, don't worry. I have no intention of telling Mom and Dad. In fact, however you came out of your room without Dad hearing? Go back in the same way." My voice was, I hoped, reassuring.

I brought the Saturn to a stop in the driveway after turning it around. I was going to go back to Brooke's. I wanted to find Alex. Then I wanted to hang out some more with Brett.

Chad grabbed one of my hands in gratitude. "Thank you, Nat. Thank you. You're, like, the best big sister ever. I swear, it was a stupid mistake and it won't happen again." He squeezed my hand for emphasis and then opened the car door.

"Chad!"

The sharpness of my voice stopped him.

"Yeah?"

I waited until he leaned back into the car before I continued. "I mean it. I'm not going to tell Mom and Dad."

"I said thank you."

"*I'm* not going to," I repeated. "*You* are."

Chapter Seventeen

It took me twenty minutes to drive back to Brooke's house—
twenty minutes of trying to figure out how I could have been
dumb enough not to see that Lisa had had her eyes on and
claws in my brother almost from the moment she'd met him. I
remembered that first Sunday in church, how she'd flirted
with him in the sanctuary and then sat close to him at lunch. I
remembered going to Kent Stevens's place for dinner and
finding the two of them together in Lisa's room.

How could I have been so blind? He was my little brother,
that was how. I still thought of him as a kid, even if he didn't
look like one. Had I been so wrapped up in my own little universe of moving and makeovers, new friends and crushes that I
hadn't thought about anyone but myself? It was bitter irony. I
had railed against moving to L.A. because I'd been so sure it
was filled with people like the one I had become.

Then I thought of my sister. She would be crushed when

she found out what happened. She'd feel totally used by Lisa, with good reason. She had been used. Lisa had used her as a way of getting to my brother.

Of course, there was no earthly requirement, and maybe not a heavenly one either, for my parents or Gemma ever to learn about Chad and Lisa. Sure, I'd told Chad that he was going to have to tell my mom and dad, but I doubted it would happen that night. My mom wasn't home, and I didn't see Chad making his confession twice. He'd probably wait until morning, at the earliest.

As I drove west on Sunset Boulevard, I wondered if maybe he didn't need to tell at all. If he outed himself, everyone would be hurt. My mom was already stressed out by her new job; my dad was happier than I'd ever seen him; Gemma would be distraught. Chad would be grounded for the rest of his life. Besides, what if he'd been telling the truth and he and Lisa really were just making a kissing video for YouTube? It was bad, yes. Chad had snuck out of the house to party. It wasn't like he'd snuck out to have *sex*.

Maybe I should just tell Lisa to stay away from my—

Crap. As I turned up into the hills toward Brooke's, I realized I'd left my cell ringer off. What if Brett had found Alex and tried to contact me?

At the next driveway, I pulled in and took my cell out of my bag. Yes, there was a text.

Not from Brett, though. From Sean.

NAT—Miss you. Lots to talk about. Word from
parentals on visit? Xo Sean

Double crap. Not tonight.

I reset the volume, then let my forehead rest for a moment on the steering wheel. Sean. One more thing I was handling badly. I texted back a quick OK and then sent one to Brett, telling him I'd had to leave the party for a bit but was on my way back, and had he found Alex? Then I got rolling again and was at the base of Brooke's driveway ten minutes later. I left my car with the valets and took another golf cart ride to the top of the hill.

That was where I found Alex. It was easy this time. She was on the White House–style columned veranda, the entryway to Brooke's house, with about ten other kids, including Brooke and Gray, but no Brett. They were partying with Jack Daniel's and Jose Cuervo. Clearly, Jack was very popular with Alex. She tipped him back and guzzled from the half-full bottle.

Triple crap.

"Nat!" She greeted me effusively, throwing her arms around me. "Hey, everyone! Look who's here! It's Natalie! She's so cool. Natalie, Natalie. Come have a drink with me, Natalie!"

She thrust the bottle at me.

I found myself slammed by thoughts.

First thought: There goes your recovery, Alex.

Second thought: Why did I ever leave this party? Why did I ever let her go off by herself? If I had stayed with her, this wouldn't have happened. I said I'd have her back. I let her down.

Third thought: It feels like I'm letting *everyone* down.

"Come on, Natalie!" Alex took a wobbly step toward me. "Have a drink!"

Brooke grinned at me, her eyes at half-mast. "Yeah, Natalie. Come on. I don't know what you do back in Minnesota, but here in California? When a friend offers you a drink, the polite thing is to take the bottle and say thank you."

I shook my head. "No thank you." I touched Alex's arm. "You don't want to do this."

She shook me off.

"I'm having fun, what's wrong with that?" She offered me the bottle again. "Just one drink. Just to show you're my friend. One drink."

"One drink, Natalie. One drink." Brooke picked up the refrain, and suddenly all the kids on the veranda were chanting it. "One drink, one drink, one drink!"

I didn't drink. Instead, I stepped toward Alex and spoke to her quietly. "We need to talk."

"No we don't." She wouldn't meet my eyes.

"Yes we do."

She smiled at me sadly. "I don't talk to friends who won't have a drink with me. Don't you respect me? I asked you so nicely. Come on. It won't kill you."

"But it might kill you," I said softly, hoping no one else could hear.

"One drink?" she whispered, tears in her eyes.

I had a choice here. I could stick to my guns and not touch the bottle of Jack. Probably Alex would be true to her word and not talk to me. Or I could take the bottle, take a swallow, and have a chance to engage her.

I chose option two.

192

"Fine. Give me the bottle."

I tilted the Jack up and let a solid swallow roll down my throat. Yeah, it burned, but there was no way I was going to sputter, or cough, or do anything that would give those kids a chance to jeer. In fact, I wiped my lips with the back of my right wrist when I was done, in what I hoped was a confident gesture. Then I put down the bottle behind me instead of giving it back to Alex.

"Yay, Natalie! You know how to drink!" Alex looked almost preternaturally happy.

Right.

"Okay," I told her. "Let's talk."

"We are talking."

"Privately?"

She shrugged and glanced over at her friends, where some guy I didn't know was doing a belly shot off Brooke's taut abs. "'Kay."

I looked for someplace to go. The front door was open. "Inside."

Alex hesitated, then shrugged. "Sounds good. Bring the Jack?"

I shook my head. She hesitated, then rolled her eyes and went inside. I followed her and sent a quick text to Brett as I walked.

Where are you?? Am with Alex. Call ASAP its crucial N

The foyer of Brooke's house made Ricardo Montalban's look like a Motel 6 lobby. Her parents apparently collected

Chinese art, since there were Ming vases on pedestals to the left and the right, lit from above by museum-quality fixtures. There was a thick wool Beijing rug in gold and blue underfoot, with a theme of fire-breathing dragons. The room was sound-proofed, too. Though the Lil Wayne blaring outside had been close to deafening, in here, once I closed the door, it was as silent as a meditation room.

"Hi," she said softly.

"Hi."

Now what? I'd never done this before. I decided to speak from my heart.

"I'm worried about you." I desperately wanted to sit on something. Anything to occupy my body. There was nothing. All we could do was stand there.

"Don't be." Her voice was gentle.

"That doesn't reassure me." I pushed some of my amazingly thick hair off my forehead, thinking that I wouldn't have had the extensions put in if it hadn't been for Alex. "What about your sobriety?"

"What about it?"

"You want to end up like your brother? A prisoner in your own house? You spent all that time in rehab," I reminded her. "You did all that work. You can still get right back on track. All this is tonight is a slip."

"No." Alex shook her head and pushed her hair out of her eyes. "A slip is when you drink so much you hit your head on some fucking monster-sized Chinese vase and bleed all over Brooke's parents new thirty-thousand-dollar living room rug. They picked it out on a trip to Hong Kong two years ago.

194

Brooke invited me. I've been to Hong Kong so many times that I took a big, fat pass." She slid down the wall, landed on her butt, and smiled up at me. "This is a drink, not a slip. And I'm not going to end up like Shep. I don't run around naked in strangers' houses."

"How about if we both just bag this party?" I suggested, resisting the temptation to remind her of some of her exploits I'd read about on the Internet. Slip, drink, whatever she thought it was, I just wanted to get her away from the alcohol.

"For sure!" she exclaimed. "Are you coming with us?"

"Huh?" I was taken aback.

"A bunch of us are going clubbing in Hollywood. Sort of like my rebirth," Alex explained. "I think you should come."

"Clubbing," I repeated, stalling for time.

"Yeah. Don't worry about ID. We know all the doormen. They love us!"

Bad to worse, I thought. At least Brooke's house was a controlled setting. Hollywood? I winced. Again, I recalled all that online research I'd done at Sandra's insistence. The escapades and the photographs. Everything. Could it be that Sandra had been right all along?

"I'm not sure clubbing is such a great idea," I said.

"Ha!" Alex barked out a laugh. "It's because you've never been. Right? You can't argue with me on that one!"

That was true. I couldn't argue with her on that one. But there were a lot of things in life I'd never done, along with at least one thing I'd done that I wished I hadn't.

"You told me about your club days. You said you didn't want to do them over again."

"That was then, this is now." She held out her hand, meaning I should take it and hoist her up.

"Alex—"

"I'm going," she insisted. "You can't stop me. A girl's allowed to have fun."

I had to stop her. But so far I wasn't doing a very good job of it, and I wasn't sure that I could do it on my own. I needed help. Where was Brett? I silently cursed him. I needed him.

I thought of the only other thing I could that might work.

"It's really okay if I go with you guys?" I asked.

Her eyes grew wide. "Really?"

"I'd love to," I lied. "That is, if it's okay with Brooke."

"You're coming? Cool!" She threw her arms around me and hugged me.

I didn't say yes, and I didn't say no. I just gave a little smile and asked where there was a bathroom. I told her that if we were going clubbing, I needed to clean up a bit. She grinned, pointed to one of the guest bathrooms, and then told me she'd be waiting outside for me.

"I'm so glad you're coming, Nat," she declared.

"Me too."

She went her way, and I went mine. I knew that what I was about to do, once I got behind the closed door of the bathroom, would be social suicide. I don't know if you've read the novel *Speak*, by Laurie Halse Anderson. Probably you have, and if you haven't, you should. In it, a girl who gets assaulted calls the cops to bust up a party and is turned into a social outcast for doing so. I hadn't been assaulted, and I wasn't calling the cops, but the operative effect of what I was about to do would be the same. Among Alex's friends, I'd be a social out-cast. But somehow, stopping Alex was way more important than having her friends, or even her, like me. Maybe once Alex sobered up, she'd thank me.

Sometimes a girl has to do what a girl has to do.

I took out my cell and speed-dialed my mom. No answer, but that made sense. She must have turned her phone off during the big church dinner. That left one other option. Yes, he was home with sick Gemma and not-so-sick Chad, but I didn't think my father would let me down. I owed it to Alex to try.

"Dad? It's me," I said when he answered his cell.

"Sweetheart! Are you okay?"

The bathroom was more like a sitting room–bathroom combination; I plopped down on a gunmetal and black fabric padded chair that had been tucked under a black vanity. "I'm okay. I'm fine. But my friend Alex—"

"What's going on?"

I told him that I'd gotten separated from Alex, that I'd found her with a bunch of her friends and a bunch of bottles, and that she was about to go clubbing. I left out my detour home with Chad and the reason for that detour. Later for that.

"I can't stop her, Dad. I tried. She asked me to help her stay sober—"

"Do you want me to try?"

I put a hand to my forehead, which was pounding. "I think so. Yeah."

"What's the address?"

I gave it to him.

"I'm on my way."

"Thanks, Dad," I told him gratefully.

My dad clicked off, and I clicked off, too. Then I heard another click—the click of the bathroom door opening a crack. Then it swung all the way open. Standing there, hands on her hips, was Brooke, with the most shit-eating grin on her face. She held a martini glass in her right hand, and she raised it to me.

"Thanks, Dad," she mimicked, with an exaggerated flat Minnesota accent.

Brooke. My social death sentence had been handed down earlier than I'd expected.

"Get out of here, Brooke." I kept my voice low.

She grinned a thousand-watt smile that never reached her cold eyes. "Get out of here? This is *my* house, and you're *my* guest last time I checked. Tell me you didn't just call your father."

I was silent.

"I *heard* you give him my address. Not that I have anything against older men, mind you. But I hear your dad's just not that hot."

Okay. That made me mad.

"Oops!" Brooke raised her eyebrows skyward. "Natalie's upset. Better leave before she calls Daddy *and* Mommy. Don't forget to wipe!"

She closed the door loudly behind her. When I was sure she was gone, I turned the knob to lock it, and then put my head in my hands.

What had I just done?

Chapter Eighteen

Pariah. Noun. 1. A person who has violated the norms and mores of a group, community, or society and as a result is rejected or turned into an outcast. 2. Me, ten minutes after I left the guest bathroom at Brooke's house and went back onto the veranda.

I took a few minutes to steel myself after Brooke closed the door, which, in retrospect, was pretty stupid. At the time, though, I thought I was helpless on my own, and knew that it would take my dad twenty minutes to get there. I went to the mirror. My cheeks were splotched red. I did some deep breathing. In, out. In, out.

Don't worry, I told myself. Your dad is coming. Alex will thank you in the morning. As for her friends, you don't really want to be friends with them anyway.

Those were the good thoughts. The bad thought was, Where's Brett? Why hasn't he called back? The only benign explanation I came up with went like this: His cell battery had died, and he'd left the party after he couldn't find me, during the time when I was driving Chad home. He didn't know my number, so he couldn't borrow someone else's cell to call me, either.

That made sense. Sort of.

I checked the time. Ten minutes since I'd called my father. I wanted to be outside when he showed up. So with one more fortifying breath, I stepped out of the bathroom and made my way through the foyer, then out the door onto the veranda. I fully expected to be met with laughs of derision. The veranda, however, was empty. Absolutely deserted, save for stray liquor bottles and cigarette butts.

Where was everyone?

Just then, a golf cart rolled into view, but it wasn't driven by one of the valets. Instead, Brooke was behind the wheel, with one bare foot up on the dashboard. She spotted me instantly and skidded to a stop in front of the shallow steps leading up to the veranda. Then she reached for a bottle of Jack at her feet. I saw that it was full, which meant it was a new bottle.

"Drink, big drinker?" she offered.

I wasn't in the mood for games. "Where's Alex?"

Brooke took a long glance left, a long glance right, a long glance up, and a long glance at the ground. "Wow. She doesn't seem to be anywhere. Where do you think she could be, Natalie? Since she doesn't seem to have waited around for you?"

I took two steps toward her. She still hadn't gotten out of the cart. "Tell me where she is, Brooke. Be a person for twenty seconds, and you'll never have to say another word to me again."

"Wow. Sounds like Natalie has a direct line to God. Or . . . maybe you *are* God! I mean, look what your mother does for a living. And you're just so *good*." She stretched languorously, then got to her feet. "Actually, Natalie? I do know where Alex is."

"Tell me," I pleaded.

She reached into the golf cart, took the key from the ignition, and tossed it to me. I grabbed for it, but it bounced off my palm and clattered to my feet.

"Drive down the hill," she suggested as I bent to retrieve the key. "Maybe she's still down there. I'd take you myself, but I'm supposed to be the host of this little get-together. Oh yeah. Say hi to your daddy, too. I hope he's bringing your pacifier."

With that, she flounced off toward the rear of her house, where the party was still going strong. In fact, I could hear the Sex Puppets crank into another of their blues-inflected tunes. Meanwhile, I stood there like an idiot, the key to the golf cart in my right hand.

Fine. I'd drive down the hill. There was only one problem. I'd never been behind the wheel of a golf cart before. So while I climbed in unafraid—it was a golf cart, after all, not a Ferrari—and found the key slot easily enough, I had no idea how to put the stupid thing into reverse. Brooke had driven it practically up to the steps, and the front wheels were two inches away from that first step. There was no way to turn it around without going backward.

One minute passed as I searched for the gearshift. Two.

Three. Finally—this is the truth—I got out of the stupid cart and literally pulled the front end around so I could get it going forward. Of course, that was when I saw the little knob that said REVERSE.

Two minutes later I was at the valet stand. I found four valets and Alex's friend Gray. From the way Gray was looking at me and shaking his head I could tell he knew why I was there. He ran a hand through his messy blond hair, his voice more sad than reproachful.

"You shouldn't have done that. Calling a parent to rescue you at a party? Maybe okay where you came from. Here? *So* not cool."

"Thanks for the advice." I swung out of the cart. "Have you seen Alex Samuels?"

He pointed his chin toward the road. "Outta here. About two minutes ago, actually. With about five other people."

My heart sank. While I had been trying to get the stupid golf cart moving, Alex had been getting into a car with whomever to go party. She'd forgotten about me.

"Where are they headed?" I asked.

"Dunno." Gray shrugged one shoulder. "I'd have gone along, but my family is flying to our villa on Lanai really early, and I hate to fly when I'm hungover. I'm going home to smoke some four twenty. The clubs'll still be here when I come back."

I had one more hope. "Alex didn't drive, did she?"

Gray laughed. "As shitfaced as she was?"

"Who did drive?"

"Brett Goldstein. Oh! Here comes my car." Gray held out

his left hand, and a valet stopped a blue BMW 320i right by it. "Good luck, Natalie. You're gonna need it."

He took the keys from the valet, gave him a buck, and drove off.

Meanwhile, I was reeling. Brett had blown me off and was *driving?* How could he do that? How could he possibly, possibly take her out clubbing? He had to know she was polluted. What did he expect her to drink in the clubs? Fiji water?

I should admit here that I was selfish enough to be hurt— and not just for Alex. I'd thought Brett was special. I'd thought he felt that way about me, too. To say I was disillusioned was an understatement. Plus my dad was coming for nothing, which meant I'd turned myself into Public Enemy #1 for nothing.

No point in calling him; I knew he wouldn't answer his cell while driving. I had no choice but to wait and tell him that the whole thing had been a huge waste. At least I saved a little time by giving my ticket to a valet. My dad would get here, I'd fill him in, I'd get in my car, and we'd caravan it home.

Fun, fun, fun.

Our Subaru beat my Saturn to the valet stand. My father rolled down the driver's side window. I must have looked as sick as I felt, because he reached a hand out before he even spoke. "I came as fast as I could. Where's your friend?"

"We're too late." His face fell, and I could see he was blaming himself. "No, no," I added quickly. "By the time I got down here, she was already gone."

"I'm so sorry. Did you try to call her?"

"Not yet," I admitted.

"Why don't you?"

"When she sees it's me, she'll never pick up."

He patted my hand. "Give it a try."

I did, even as the Saturn was pulled up behind my dad's car. As I'd predicted, my call went straight to voice mail. I tried Brett's cell, too, just to say I did. Same thing.

That was it. There was nothing else I could do. Which was exactly what my dad told me before he uttered the nicest four words I'd heard all day.

"Sweetheart? Let's go home."

I nodded and headed for my car. Going home was what I wanted more than anything in the world. Except for rolling back the clock and stopping Alex from doing whatever she was doing right now.

Chapter Nineteen

I've had some terrible nights in my life, but the one of Brooke's party was right down there on the Y-axis.

After we got home—my mom was still at her church thing—I turned down my dad's offer to dig into some Häagen-Dazs. Instead, I went straight to my room and took the hottest shower in the history of hot showers, cranking up the Mr. Steam for good measure, until I felt as dehydrated physically as I did mentally. Then I drank huge gulps of cold water straight from the tap, made a desultory effort to dry off, and crawled into bed.

Sleep was not my friend. I lay there, staring at the shadows on my ceiling created by moonlight slanting in through the custom-made blinds. All I could think about was how royally I had screwed up my life.

There was Chad's escapade. Should I tell my parents? Should I make Chad tell them? Had he defied my expectations and already told them? If he had, what would happen next?

There was Sean, the Great Non-Communicator. Why did it have to be after we'd had sex that I realized he might well never be the emotional partner I now longed for? We'd been just fine before. He was reliable. He was steady. He went to church and believed in God. Was it him or me with whom I was unhappy? As I lay against my pillows in the moonlight, I admitted to myself that the latter was a definite possibility.

There was Brett. One minute I was the focus of his attention, the next he was blowing me off to go party with polluted Alex in Hollywood. Who does that?

Alex. Thinking about her was the hardest of all. I should have stuck to her like Elmer's once I knew she was drinking. I figured out why she had left without me: she didn't really want me clubbing, because she knew I'd bitch at her about alcohol. I had a vision of her just before I fell into a fitful sleep: on a nightclub dance floor, her blouse spinning in one hand overhead, her La Perla bra spinning in the other.

I had the same vision on waking up; my alarm sounded at eight, since I'd stupidly forgotten to turn it off.

Even before brushing my teeth, I went to my laptop. I had an email to send—to Sean, letting him know that I wanted to talk with him about his upcoming visit.

As my laptop booted, I opened the window shades; it was another glorious California.

Sunday. Church day. Fair enough. I could use it. Two hummingbirds buzzed around the feeder, taking dive-bomb runs at each other, swooping out of the way and then coming back for more. I watched, mesmerized. What would it be like to be one of those birds? To worry only about getting enough nectar in your system to power your fluttering wings, day after day after

206

day? Would it be boring, or just fine? Just fine, I decided. After all, you'd have a brain the size of a pinprick. About the level at which my brain had been operating lately, come to think of it.

When I went to my email, I saw a message with an attachment waiting for me. From Chad. The text was short.

> Sis—I wasn't lying about the video. Check it
> out. Chad

The attachment was two minutes long. It was of Chad and Lisa in the cabana at Brooke's party. He hadn't been lying: it was a tongue-in-cheek, so to speak, instructional video on how to kiss. Lisa offered commentary to the camera about lips, slobbering and the lack thereof, tongue penetration and the lack thereof, and the importance of coming up for air, with Chad occasionally coming into frame. At first he played a rank amateur kisser who didn't know what he was doing. Once trained by Lisa, he became a champion lip-locker.

Okay. I had to admit it. It was funny. It would have been even funnier if it hadn't been my thirteen-year-old-but-looks-sixteen-years-old brother. It wasn't at all what I'd feared. How would that impact my telling, or my asking Chad to tell, our parents? Hard to say. I'd think about that some more after I wrote the email to Sean.

> Dear Sean,
> It's me. I've been a jerk. I hope you can
> forgive me. I know it has been hard for us to
> talk by phone and by Skype. You must feel

*like I am pushing you to talk more openly
with me, because I feel like I'm pushing you,
too. I do think that being able to talk openly
is our best hope now that we're a couple of
thousand miles apart. But that doesn't mean
that it's going to be easy. That I'm confused
about what happened between us at the lake
house hasn't made things easier. So I hope
that when you actually come*

My cell rang. I stopped writing. It was a blocked number.

"Hello?"

"Nat?" I didn't recognize the female voice.

"Yes, it's Nat."

"It's Sandra. Did you hear the news?"

"Oh, hi! Sorry, I didn't recognize your voice." I felt a little burst of adrenaline. From the tone of her voice, I could tell that whatever the news was, it wasn't good. "What news?"

"Your new best friend, Alex Samuels?"

"What about her?" My heart pounded against my rib cage.

"Evidently, she was at a party at Brooke Summers's house, and then she went clubbing with a bunch of kids. They were all roasted and toasted, which doesn't surprise me. Anyway, they got into an accident at the corner of Hollywood and Highland. She's in the hospital. Cedars-Sinai. One other kid is there, too."

Oh no.

"Who's the other kid?"

"Brett something-or-other. I don't know him." Sandra

went on, with a tone of superiority, "Not that I'd want to know him."

Brett and Alex. Both in the hospital. Oh no, oh no, oh no.

"How did you find out?"

"Tracy McFarlane's mom is a nurse at Cedars. She called Tracy, and Tracy called me. There's a story about it on *TMZ*. I thought you'd want to know."

What could I say? "Thanks, Sandra."

"Don't mention it. See you in church later. Bye."

She clicked off, which was good, because I was literally speechless. Numbly, I saved the Sean email and went to the *TMZ* website.

There it was, on the home page, about halfway down: CLUB KIDS INJURED IN HOLLYWOOD WRECK. The piece was short, only a few paragraphs, but it confirmed what Sandra had reported. Alex was in the hospital, in serious condition. Brett, too, in fair condition.

Crap.

I pulled on a Viterbo University sweatshirt with the sleeves cut off and a pair of khaki cargo pants and ran downstairs. Fortunately, my sister and brother were still sleeping, so I didn't have to deal with the Chad thing immediately. But my mom and dad were both in the kitchen. Dad was cooking an omelette breakfast, while my mom was at the table, engrossed in a phone conversation with a congregant. I padded in and went straight for the coffeemaker.

"Morning, Nat," my dad greeted me. "Cheese omelette? Or cheese-and-shiitake-'shrooms?"

"Just coffee, thanks," I told him as I poured myself a steaming mug. My hands shook so much the coffee sloshed around. I don't usually drink coffee black, but since that was the color of my mood, it seemed fitting. I sat down across from my mom, who gave me a little wave, then went right back to her call. She was already dressed for church, in a black skirt, a white blouse, and a beige jacket. Stylish, but not too stylish. People don't like it when their minister looks better than they do.

"Uh-huh," my mom said into her cell. "Well, I'm supposed to be at the building by . . . uh-huh. This takes priority. . . . Uh-huh . . . uh-huh . . . I'll see you in forty-five minutes. But I can't stay long. I have a service to run."

Forty-five minutes. There was no place in Los Angeles you could get to in less than twenty minutes. Huh. She was out of there. When I told the story, I'd have to talk fast.

She clicked off. "Congregant emergency. They call; Marsha Shelton answers. The day gets off to a catastrophic start."

I sipped my coffee as my father joined us at the table. Maybe he'd told my mom about the night before. Maybe not. I'd find out soon enough. "Alex was in a car accident last night."

"Oh no!" my mother exclaimed. She and my father shared a look. "What happened? Your dad told me a little about the party."

Very quickly, I sketched out what I knew, leaving out the part about Chad's being at that party. My mother preferred conversations with a single topic.

"And it's my fault," I concluded, glum. "I shouldn't have let her out of my sight. I would have been the designated driver. How could I have been so stupid?" Now I was on the verge of tears.

I saw my mother frown. I don't like it when my mom frowns.

"What?" I asked.

"First of all," my mother began, "Alex is responsible for Alex's choices, not you."

"But I—"

"*Not you*," she repeated firmly. "I remember sitting with you on the floor not very long ago, talking about Alex, whether you should be her friend or not."

"I remember, too."

She tugged unconsciously at the cuffs of her blouse. "Clearly, you decided it was a good idea."

I stared into my coffee. "Yeah. I did."

"Any regrets now?"

I snuck a glance at my dad, but he was letting my mom take the lead. "All kinds of regrets," I admitted.

"Do your regrets outweigh the good part of your friendship with her?" My mother's eyes bored into me.

Tough question. No. I didn't think so. Even with her in the hospital.

"No," I declared.

She shook her head and frowned more deeply. "Well, that's something that I think you're going to need to reexamine. I'm not telling you what the right answer is. She's your friend, not mine. You know Alex far better than I do. I *can* tell you that looking from the outside, I don't think you have had the kind of influence on her that you hoped."

211

My dad nodded. "You think you could have been the designated driver? You also could have been in the seat next to her."

Ouch. I heard what they were saying. It hurt.

Mom stood. "I've got to go. Natalie, we can talk again at church, if you want."

I stood, too. "I'm missing church today. I'm going to the hospital. I'm taking the Saturn, if that's okay."

It was unusual to miss church. But it was okay, which tells you something about my mom and dad. I grabbed my bag and the car keys and beat my mother out the door.

Chapter Twenty

I was planning to drive straight to Cedars-Sinai, but then I remembered that Alex's brother, Shepard, was under house arrest, meaning he wouldn't be permitted even to see his sister. I had mixed feelings about this. I thought that Shepard was lucky to be under house arrest for his drug conviction, instead of in prison. Someone poorer, who couldn't hire a first-rate lawyer, wouldn't have the option. So Shepard, except for his naked wanderings into neighbors' houses and even bedrooms, was basically confined to the world's ritziest penal facility, namely, the Samuelses' family manse.

And yet . . . what would have been so bad about letting him pay for a police escort so he could see his sister in the hospital? He had to be worried sick, which was exactly why I made a detour to the Samuelses' front door.

When I got there, I found a small army of Latino groundskeepers and landscapers, cutting grass, trimming hedges, edging the lawn, blowing leaves, and planting new beds of flowers. These landscaping teams were as ubiquitous to Beverly Hills as the snow was to Mankato.

When Shepard opened the double French front doors for me, he was freshly shaved and wore a pair of jeans with an aquamarine golf shirt. To my surprise, he'd also cut his hair. Basically, he was barely recognizable as the stoned, naked guy I'd found in my bed.

"Come in, Nat," he urged, ushering me inside. There was a small, airy sitting room just beyond the front door, with a glass wall that looked out onto the canyon, and that was where we installed ourselves on a couple of burgundy leather-bound chairs. I saw new worry lines, like quote marks, between his eyebrows.

"I've been on the phone all morning with Cedars-Sinai. She's in a private room on the sixth floor." He rubbed his forehead as he talked. "I haven't told Chloe. But I'm afraid that some other kid at camp will hear about it and start blabbing."

"It's hard to know the right thing to do," I said sympathetically. "How is Alex?"

Shepard stood and paced with nervous energy. "She ruptured her spleen. The doctors removed it last night. She's got contusions on her legs, and possibly a bruised pancreas, which could cause all kinds of problems down the road. Right now, she's allegedly 'resting comfortably,'" he added bitterly. He smacked one fist into an open palm. "I cannot believe that I have to do all this by phone!"

"I'm heading over there now. I'll find out everything I can," I promised, standing up. A lump rose in my throat.

"I'm sorry," I said softly. "I could have stopped this from happening."

He smiled at me with kind eyes. "You *think* you could have stopped this from happening."

"I know I could have," I insisted. "I promised I'd help her stay sober—"

"Ha!" he barked, following it with rueful laughter.

"What's so funny?"

He wagged a finger at me. "You. You're funny. You clearly don't have a lot of contact with people who end up in rehab."

"That's true," I admitted. "But—"

"But nothing. You're talking to someone who has been in rehab three times, and clearly the third time *wasn't* the charm." To illustrate his point, he tapped one bare foot against the ankle bracelet that let law enforcement monitor his whereabouts every hour of every day. "Now go. Call me when you can, okay?"

I reached for my purse, which I'd left on the chair, and looped the strap over my shoulder as I stood. "I'll definitely call you from the hospital—"

"Oh!" he exclaimed, holding up a palm. "I just thought of something. Wait here."

Without giving me a chance to respond, he bounded out of the room. There was nothing I could do but wait, so I turned to the picture window and took in the magnificence of the canyon. A red-tailed hawk was tracing lazy circles across the sky. But honestly, I barely saw it. I was still rethinking the night before. What I had done. What I hadn't. Mostly what I hadn't.

"I do that, too." I spun back to see Shepard in the doorway, a melancholy smile on his face. "Stare out that window," he said, cocking his chin toward the glass. I saw he now held a framed photograph and a small white stuffed animal in his hands.

"Yeah," was all I managed to say.

"I have a couple of things that Alexis would probably like in her room," he explained. "If you wouldn't mind . . ." He moved toward me and offered the photograph. "Our mom and dad."

I took it. It was a picture of Mr. and Mrs. Samuels in their thirties, on a photographic safari in Africa. They had multiple cameras around their necks, arms around each other, huge smiles on their sunburnt faces. They were obviously in love.

What a tragedy. What a terrible, terrible tragedy.

"Yeah," Shepard said, as if reading my mind. "It pretty much ruined everything there was to ruin. And then some." He looked down at his other hand and seemed almost surprised to see the stuffed animal. "Ah! And this is Twitch. Alexis always loved Twitch. I don't think she's ever slept a night away from him. Even when we travel. This rabbit ought to have a passport."

He gave me the bunny. No bigger than eight inches and well worn, it was missing a button eye, and the monofilament whiskers that had obviously once adorned the head had diminished to one thin strand that brushed my forefinger.

"My dad brought that back for her when she was five, from a business trip." Shepard smiled at the memory. "I think he brought me a new guitar. The littler the kid, the cheaper the present. But they don't love it any less." He thrust his hands into the pockets of his jeans.

"I wish you could come with me," I told him.

"I wish it, too."

He turned away and I took that as a cue not to stare. Maybe he was getting ready to cry. Maybe he was crying already.

"I should go."

"Thanks, Nat. Alexis is lucky to have you as a friend."

He still didn't look at me. I said goodbye and found my way out.

It took me just a half hour to get to Cedars-Sinai, and five minutes more to find a spot in the parking structure. I wished it had taken longer, since I was still trying to figure out what to say to Alex when I saw her. Also, what I'd say to Brett. Because as guilty as I felt about Alex, that was how pissed I was at Brett.

Cedars-Sinai is a huge hospital. I got lost twice trying to get to the sixth floor, because I didn't realize that there were multiple sixth floors in multiple buildings. It was only by the process of elimination that I found the one with Alex's private room. As for Brett, he was being held mostly for observation on the neuropsych floor. His CAT scan looked fine, but since he'd banged his head, they were watching for signs of a subdural hematoma or a concussion. All this I got from a too-helpful Filipina nurse at the desk who, to my benefit, had only a tenuous grasp on the notion of patient privacy.

"Alex Samuels?"

"Room 614, at the end of the corridor," she told me.

"Thanks."

As I started down the hallway, I took out the photograph and the toy rabbit. I thought Alex might be happy if I came with both these things visible. I'd already decided what my approach would be. Supportive. Kind. I couldn't reject her for what she'd done, and I wasn't going to go all heavy on her. Though I don't believe that the Almighty punishes us for our misdeeds and misjudgments, at least not in obvious ways, it did seem to me that this accident was punishment enough.

I don't know why—I do know why: I was incredibly naïve—I figured that because Alex's parents were dead and her brother was under house arrest, she would have no other visitors on this Sunday morning and I would be able to stroll right into her room. Color me stupid. There was a big cluster of teens in the hallway outside Alex's room, all of whom I recognized from Brooke's party.

So not good, especially when Brooke and Gray peeled off and stepped toward me when I was maybe twenty feet from the door. As they approached, I wondered why Gray was here. Wasn't he jetting off to Hawaii or something?

"Hi," he offered without enthusiasm.

Brooke offered no greeting. Instead, she stared at me as if I was dripping raw sewage.

Fine. I would ignore her. I kept my eyes on Gray. "I thought you were going to Hawaii."

"If you haven't heard, my friends were in a car accident. I changed my plans."

I nodded. "How's Alex?"

He shrugged. "Jacked up, but she'll live."

"I want to see her," I declared.

He shook his head. "Bad idea."

"What do you mean, bad idea? Are the doctors with her now?"

"Nope. It's just a bad idea."

"Oh, come on, Gray," Brooke interrupted. "Tell the truth. We don't want this twit around, Alex doesn't want this twit around, and if this twit had any sense, she would get her twitty fat ass out of here before something bad happens."

"Are you *threatening* me?" I couldn't believe it.

She gave me a smug smile. "What do you think?"

Okay. That was it. I was in no mood for the bullcrap of Brooke of Beverly Hills.

I moved within spitting distance of her and locked eyes with her. "Screw you."

I ignored their looks of shock, dodged around them, and moved at double time toward the door. I was going into Alex's room, and it didn't matter what Brooke or Gray or anyone else had to say about it.

As I neared the door, the teen assemblage stared. The word was obviously out about how I had called my father, and they all hated me for it. Fine. I could deal. I did deal, until I reached a nurse blocking the open door. She was imposingly big, with cropped gray hair and a no-nonsense manner.

"Where do you think you're going?"

"To see my friend Alex." I tried to make my voice friendly.

She shook her head. "No you aren't. Three visitors at a time, and there are already four. Wait your turn like everyone else."

I peered into the room past her but I couldn't see Alex;

the curtain was drawn around her bed. I could hear quiet talking and laughter from the other side.

I looked at the framed photograph in my hand and Twitch, the stuffed rabbit. For a moment, I thought about asking Nurse Ratched to give them to Alex, but then thought better of it. Shepard had asked me to give these things to her, not to transmit them via some anonymous nurse.

I turned around and trudged past the knot of Alex's party friends, back toward the elevators.

"Buh-bye," Brooke jeered, waggling her fingers at me as I passed her.

I whirled. "What is your problem?"

She gave me an evil smile. "Where ya headed?"

"I'm going to see Brett. I have a few things I want to tell him," I muttered.

"That he needs to go to driving school?"

"That he needs not to drink if he's going to drive, for starters."

"Aren't *we* sanctimonious? I think we should start calling you the Virginator. It's perfect for you."

I wished it *was* the perfect name for me. But I wasn't nearly as good or pure as she thought I was. Suddenly, she laughed.

"What's so funny?" I asked, challenging her.

"You're so sure Brett was drunk," she surmised.

"Logical conclusion, don't you think?" I snapped. I was getting tired of this conversation.

"Sure is." She laughed again. "If it were true. But when you talk to him—*if* you talk to him—he'll tell you that Alex barfed on his lap while he was making a left turn. That's when the van hit him. Kinda ruined his shirt and jeans, but hey, that's the way it goes. Oh! They want me in there now." She waved back toward Alex's room, where someone was now exiting. "Gotta go. Bye, Virginator. Love ya. Mean it."

She took off, leaving me alone in the hallway.

Could that even be true? There was only one way to find out.

I went down to the fourth floor to find Brett. Again, I didn't get what I wanted. The door to his room was closed. A nurse told me that he was in with the doctors and his parents, and though I waited for a half hour, no one went in and no one came out.

Finally, I gave up and left, the framed photograph and Twitch still in my arms.

Chapter Twenty-One

The praying thing.

To tell you the truth, it's often been a problem for me. It's not one I talk about much, being the daughter of a minister and all. My parents have always said, "You can talk to us about anything," and I know they mean it. That doesn't mean, though, that there aren't consequences to sharing things. It's the main reason, as you know, that I'm not talking with them about Sean. Same thing, in a different way, about prayer. How would they feel if I said that sometimes prayer seems like a big fat hypocritical waste of time?

When I'm feeling that way, I go through the motions. I'm in the pew on Sunday with the rest of my family, eyes closed at the appropriate times, singing at an appropriate volume, and even creating blessings and beseechings if asked to do so, like at a church youth group meeting. All the while, here's what I'm thinking: Why should God listen to me, a seventeen-year-old girl with a privileged American life, while there are probably seven billion people out there living not-so-privileged lives? Shouldn't he be paying them a lot more attention than me?

Besides, what if God really *did* answer my prayer? Would that mean that he is waiting for me to pray to him and won't help unless I do pray to him? Does doing bad things mean that he will listen to me less, or listen to me more? Ditto doing good things? If there's a tornado and one guy's house is flattened, while his neighbor's house is untouched, does that mean God likes the guy whose house is fine more than the other guy? Finally, can you *really* petition the Lord with prayer?

Now, that said, there are plenty of times when I have faith. True faith, in God as the divine and Jesus as my personal savior. But I'd be lying if I said that there weren't times when I should be praying and instead these questions slam into each other in my mind like subatomic particles in a supercollider.

How do I deal with those times? It's not easy. Sometimes I work on song lyrics. All I can say is it's no wonder that most songs are about falling in love and having your heart broken, and not about huge questions about the Almighty. There's a reason why much of Christian rock—some of which is really good—doesn't ask many questions about faith. It just assumes you know the answer.

How was I when I left Cedars-Sinai? I wanted to pray. Strike that. I *needed* to pray. That was why when I left with the ugly stares from Alex's friends still fresh on my soul, I drove the fifteen minutes to the Church of Beverly Hills.

There were a thousand people there for services, but everyone was in the sanctuary when I arrived. The halls were eerily empty; I had no intention of slipping into the sanctuary to join the throng. I had another destination in mind.

For an edifice that was over the top in many ways, the Church of Beverly Hills had a chapel that was a bit of a throwback to a simpler time. Located in a separate building behind the main structure, it had seating for no more than seventy-five people, in a semicircle of rough-hewn Lebanon cedar (shipped from that nation, by the by) wooden pews, the planks of the seats covered by soft red cushions. The walls were also cedar, set with narrow strips of wood in a crosshatch pattern that narrowed as they got closer to the ceiling, almost as if the designer was implying that the congregation's prayers would come together as they rose toward heaven. I'm not sure that you would call the stage of this chapel a proper chancel, since it was raised only a few inches above the main floor. But that was how I thought of it, and I loved that it held just a couple of wooden lecterns and a light-blond upright piano with a matching bench.

All the times I'd come to the church, I'd never seen anyone in the chapel. That was why I went straight to it after I parked the Saturn. I sat not in a pew, but on the edge of the chancel. I leaned forward, put my elbows on my thighs, my head in my hands, and squeezed my eyes so tightly shut that my photoreceptors activated and I saw geometric patterns not unlike those on the chapel walls.

I prayed. To Jesus. To whatever God might be, however he might be listening.

I prayed that Alex would find the strength and support she needed to keep herself safe and on a path toward the Almighty. Even if she hated churches.

I prayed that the story Brooke had recounted about Brett was true, because that could mean that he had taken it upon himself to be the designated driver for the night.

I prayed that Chad would come to understand that just because your body was that of an adult, it didn't mean that you should do adult things.

I prayed that Gemma wouldn't get too flipped out because her new best friend was oh-so-clearly ready to seduce her little brother.

I prayed that my mom wouldn't get too burned out, and that my dad could adjust to my mother's new schedule.

I prayed that this whole Los Angeles thing would work out for all of us.

Then I added a few words on my own behalf. I reminded myself of what I had prayed about for my brother, and added that knowing the right thing to do—such as not having sex with Sean—and actually doing the right thing were not the same. I prayed for guidance. Wisdom. And some kind of clarity about my life.

I prayed again that my prayers weren't selfish. Please. Let them not be selfish.

Then I opened my eyes and saw I was not alone.

Someone I knew was sitting at the end of the pew nearest to me, her legs up on the wood. She'd moved three cushions behind her head and had the slightest smile on her open face. She wore a short black skirt and a long-sleeved gray silk blouse with embroidery around the sweetheart neckline. On her feet were a pair of black strappy sandals.

It was Mia, the girl I'd met on the songwriters' night. The same girl I'd watched with Alex on *In and Out*. The girl whose father was Big Jam.

I'd thought I would never see her again.

"Hi, Nat." Her smile was as friendly as when I'd first met her.

"You remembered my name." I stretched my arms overhead and shook out my hands. My head had been resting in them for so long that the right one had fallen slightly asleep. "I remember you, too. You're Mia. Welcome back."

"Thanks."

"I know who you are," I said boldly, getting to my feet.

Her shoulders hunched forward. "You saw *In and Out*."

"Yeah."

"Amazing what you can learn from watching TV." Mia stood, too. "Listen, are you busy now?"

"Not really."

"Then why don't we go for coffee or something? I don't know about you, but I kind of think chapels are sacred."

I grinned. "Are we going to have a profane conversation?"

"Only if you're extremely, extremely lucky. Do you know Café Med?"

I didn't.

She hitched a thumb toward her shoulder. "It's at the corner of Hip and Groovy, better known as Sunset Plaza on Sunset Boulevard. Follow me there."

• • •

Café Med turned out to be an Italian-themed bistro in West Hollywood with a sidewalk café attached, and was exactly as Mia had implied. Hip. And groovy. As we approached the terrace from the parking lot behind the building, nearly every seat was filled by willowy size-nothing girls whose cheekbones weighed more than they did (the models), nearly-as-skinny and nearly-as-gorgeous girls a few inches shorter (the actresses), and their male equivalents (the model-actors). There was one empty table at the east end of the patio, and a very tall, very thin Italian hostess with hair that needed no extensions led us to it. Next to her, Mia—who couldn't have been bigger than five foot two—was positively dwarfed.

A buff Italian waiter with short dark hair and green eyes appeared immediately. He offered us menus, but Mia ordered bruschetta, a calzone, and two Diet Cokes, telling me to trust her. Maybe this was a Los Angeles tradition. I remembered Alex doing the same thing at the Ivy. From the approving look the waiter gave her, I knew she'd ordered well. He poured us two glasses of ice water and hustled off to the kitchen.

"I'm guessing you didn't come back to the church to see me," I told Mia when he'd departed, "seeing as how I had no idea I would be here until about fifteen minutes beforehand."

"You were a woman with a plan. I'm guessing you needed to pray. Why?"

Why indeed. Realizing the irony—that I was the stranger everyone told their life story to, and here I was with a girl I barely knew and wanted to talk to—I found myself spilling

227

everything that had happened with Alex and Brett. It was a relief to tell somebody. Fortunately, Mia was a patient listener.

"Wow." Mia looked thoughtful. "That basically really sucks."

That made me laugh. "Well put. Now you. What were you doing there?"

Mia leaned back in her chair. "Well, I've decided to join."

"That's great!"

She ran a forefinger over the condensation on her water glass. "Here's why. When I met you in the sanctuary that night? I felt—I don't know, it's hard to describe—safe."

Safe. I liked that. "I'm glad. You're going to like my mom."

Mia nodded thoughtfully. "Yeah. She's the minister with the talk show. I've done my homework."

I was proud of myself. Even after *In and Out,* I hadn't Googled Mia. That doesn't mean I wasn't tempted to, though.

"Did you do your homework on me?" Mia asked.

"Just *In and Out.*" It felt great to be truthful.

Mia laughed warmly. "That? That's TV, not homework."

The hot waiter brought our food, redolent of garlic and fresh basil. Since we were sharing, he made a big show of cutting the calzone in two with a gleaming knife and placing the halves on our respective plates. "Beautiful girls deserve a beautiful presentation," he intoned with a thick accent.

Okay. To be called a beautiful girl on the terrace of Café Med, terrace of the truly beautiful girls? That was fun, too.

"What didn't I learn from *In and Out?*" I forked a piece of the calzone into my mouth. Scrumptious.

Mia looked wistful. "A lot. They didn't want to make the show a total downer."

"This is Hollywood. Everyone has a story." I thought of Alex in the hospital.

"Not like mine," Mia declared.

For a moment, she hesitated. Like telling me what she was about to tell me was a big decision.

Oh no, I thought. Not another girl who just got out of rehab.

That wasn't it, though. Not by a long shot. In many ways, rehab was a picnic compared to Mia's story.

"Three months ago I was living with my mother over the hill in Sherman Oaks. Taking care of her while I was in high school, actually. She taught English before she got sick. Now she's dead, and I'm living with the father I didn't even know I had, in a mansion so big that my room is about the size of my old apartment." Mia smiled sadly. "You can reattach your jaw to your face now."

She had related her story matter-of-factly, but it was still shocking.

"I'm sorry." My voice was a whisper.

"Breast cancer, since you're going to ask. It only took a year from start to finish."

How horrible. How absolutely, gut-wrenchingly horrible. To lose your mother when you were still a kid. I couldn't imagine. It reminded me of Alex. Look at what I'd been praying about. This was just the kind of thing I thought God ought to be paying attention to, not the tawdry details of my stable little life.

That was exactly what I told Mia. All she did was shrug and say she didn't quite have that figured out, either.

"But you still want to join a church," I prompted her.

"Of course. Why wouldn't I?"

Something didn't make sense to me. "You guys had a church in the Valley, didn't you?"

She nodded.

"Why change?"

She stabbed a piece of calzone and swirled it in the tomato sauce on her plate. "It would have just been too hard to stay. All those people with pity and sadness on their faces. The funeral was there. I went back a few times after she died. It was more than I could bear. Really."

I frowned. It reminded me a little of what Sandra had told me about her former life in New York. "I would have thought the community would be comforting. That's what my mom always says."

"Your mom wasn't sixteen when her mother died of breast cancer," Mia said bluntly. She took a long swallow of Diet Coke.

"It's funny," I mused. "Strange funny, not funny funny. I'm not really big into the celeb thing, but I think I would have heard about Big Jam's wife dying. It would have been on the news."

Mia gave a short laugh. "It would have. But since they weren't married, and I didn't know he was my father until the last two months my mom was alive, that would have been a little tough."

Wow.

I drank some water. Ate some of the bruschetta. And waited what I hoped was an appropriate length of time before speaking again. "Who did your mother say your dad was all those years? She must have told you something."

"She did," Mia acknowledged. "She said she had a one-night stand when she was in college, back before she came to Jesus. She said that the guy stayed a sinner, so she wasn't interested in a relationship with him."

"Is that the truth?" I asked.

She looked thoughtful. "James is . . . I guess I don't know what he is yet."

"James?"

"Big Jam's real name, which you won't hear in the media either," Mia explained. "No way can I call him Big Jam, and I'm definitely not ready to call him Dad. So it's James kinda by default."

We ate in silence for a few minutes as I digested what Mia had told me. She was living with a father that a few months earlier she hadn't even known she had. Not just *a* father. *Big Jam.*

How weird was that?

The conversation shifted. Mia started asking me questions. Did I have a boyfriend back in Mankato? Had I made any friends out here? How did I feel about the move to Los Angeles?

I, the girl who everyone talks to, talked for a half hour straight. I talked about everything except having sex with Sean the night before we'd come. Just as it had felt great to tell Mia about Alex and Brett, it felt good to share my experience and my feelings about my new life. Still, I knew it would also feel good to share the truth about Sean with someone. Why not this girl, after everything she had just shared with me?

Tell her, I told myself.

I knew I should. I knew I could. She would understand.

I didn't. I wasn't ready. I'm not proud of this, but I didn't know then if I would ever be ready.

Instead, I polished off the rest of my calzone and took another bite of bruschetta. "Can I ask you something else?"

"Sure."

"How'd you get through it?"

"You mean, with my mom?"

I nodded. "Yeah. Your mom and everything else, pretty much."

"Pretty much on faith," she admitted, echoing how I had put it.

"Faith," I repeated. "That doesn't make a whole lot of sense."

She rubbed her chin thoughtfully. "You're right. It doesn't. But if I'd paid attention to reason, I would have been out partying with Alex and Brett last night, too. I've earned it, I'd say."

She stared pensively out at the beautiful day and then around the patio at the beautiful people eating lunch. "I suppose faith never makes sense, really. It's something your heart tells you is true. You can't prove it, but you believe anyway. And sometimes, Natalie?" Her eyes met mine. "Sometimes faith is all we've got."

Chapter Twenty-Two

When I drove home in record time—Sunday traffic in Los Angeles is pleasantly manageable—I had Mia's cell number in my phone, and she had mine. It felt great. I had a new friend who—she told me as much—was opposed to drinking, drugging, smoking, and doing the deed, at least for herself. Before I arrived at the gate to Ricardo's mansion, I got my first text from her.

LOVED TODAY. SEE U THERE NEXT WEEK AND
HOPEFULLY WED FOR MOVIE. CALL ME LTR.

It was so thoughtful. She knew I'd be looking for her and would be disappointed if I didn't see her. As for getting together before the next Sunday, a new Judd Apatow movie had just opened, and I figured that by midweek the rush to see it would be mostly over. We'd discussed maybe going to the

Grove. I smiled at the thought, for two reasons. First, because two weeks earlier, I hadn't had any idea what the Grove was. Second, if I was thinking about the movies, I had to be feeling better about life.

When I reached the top of the driveway, I saw that we had a visitor; a black Range Rover was parked next to my parents' Subaru. A vanity license plate announced to the world who was behind the wheel.

KSTEVE. Kent Stevens. Father of Lisa Hot-for-Chad Stevens.

Before I even shut down the Saturn, I guessed the sequence of events that had unfolded in my absence. My brother had gone to my father and told him what had happened the night before. My father had called my mother. They'd had a serious three-way yak. Kent Stevens had been summoned for a postchurch discussion, because my mom and dad believed that when kids were involved in something potentially dangerous—sneaking out to a high school party and making a video would fit that definition—not only did all the parents have a right to know, but it was the responsibility of other parents to tell them.

I'm not saying this is right or wrong. I'm saying this is the way it is with them. I learned the hard way in Mankato, when I made the mistake of hitchhiking with my friend Shelby instead of calling for a ride. Someone in our church saw us and phoned my parents, who then called Shelby's mom and dad. By the time I got home, all four parents were waiting for us. Big fun. Note to reader: if you live in a small town, you already know you can't get away with anything.

There was only one piece of the puzzle missing, I thought,

as I closed the door to the Saturn. My folks liked to have all the players present at these kinds of crisis meetings, and I was definitely one of the players in this sordid passion play. Why hadn't I been summoned? I checked my cell again to see if there was something I'd missed. Nope. I'd been left out of the loop somehow.

Where would the summit be taking place? My best guess was the kitchen, so I decided to go around and in via the back deck so I could avoid the encounter group. During the day, the sliding doors were usually unlocked.

That was the plan. It survived until I approached the deck and heard my mother and Kent Stevens talking.

Now, I am not by nature an eavesdropper, but Kent was yakking so loud it couldn't be helped. As for my mother, her own decibel level was a standard deviation above normal. In short, he was pissed, and so was she. As I listened, though, I was surprised to figure out that their mutual ire had nothing to do with my brother and Kent's daughter. It was about church business. Normally, this would be of mere academic interest, but the kinds of threats Kent was making made it matter a lot more than that.

"I'm giving you one more chance to reconsider, Marsha. I want the sanctuary and social hall a week from today for my niece's wedding. I *need* it." Kent said the word "need" in the same tone that a Mafia boss might use to say he needed his blackmail money paid immediately. Or else.

"I know that's how you feel, Kent. I'd like you to have it." My mother's voice was understanding but firm. "But they're both booked. Alcoholics Anonymous is having their annual conference. We've donated the space, and they're expecting a thousand people. A hundred of them are members of our church family."

"Then I'll rent them other space for their damn meeting!" Kent was adamant. "This is my niece. She was going to elope. When my sister found out, she threw a fit. No daughter of hers is going to elope. You wouldn't want her to elope, either," he added. "You'd want her to have a church wedding."

"Of course I do. I wish I could officiate, too. But I'm booked to keynote at the conference. I'm sorry, Kent, but the space just isn't available."

"Are you deaf? I just said I'll rent them another place to meet!" Kent fairly exploded.

"They don't want another place to meet. They want our church, they reserved it, and they deserve to be in a house of God. From what I understand, you took part in the board vote that approved this rental. In fact, you voted yes."

I edged closer to the house, not wanting to be seen.

"I don't get it, Marsha." Kent's tone changed. He sounded almost regretful. "Stuff like this comes up all the time. Our last minister would have been happy to do this. We've always been a church that puts its membership first. A church that goes out of the way for its membership. I want Skyler and Paul to have a church wedding. In our church."

Silence. As if my mom was actually thinking about it.

"I'm sorry, Kent. There's nothing I can do."

Kent's tone was light in response. "I understand your position, though you're making it hard for me—which means it might be harder for your husband's novel to become a film, or for Gemma to have a chance to be on my show, or any number of things. You understand that."

Shut the front door. He'd really take back the goodie basket unless Mom fell into line?

Kent didn't know my mother like I did. If he had, he would have recognized the venom in her voice when she responded with utter calm to his obvious threats. "You do what you need to do, Kent. I have to look at myself in the mirror in the morning."

The producer barked a short laugh. "So do I. Goodbye, Marsha."

The conversation was obviously over, so I hightailed it around the house and through the front door before Kent made his way back to his Range Rover. Now I had to decide whether to tell my mom that I'd overheard the conversation.

As it turned out, I didn't have to. She called for me as I reached the bottom of the steps to the second floor. "Nat! Can I talk to you for a moment?"

I turned and trudged back toward her. She wore the same work clothes I'd seen her in at breakfast.

"Natalie?"

"Yeah?"

"Sometime in the not-too-distant future, when you pick your beautiful career, please don't try to be Harriet the Spy."

Yikes. She must have seen me as I eavesdropped. How?

"Your shadow," she said by way of explanation. "On the patio. Fortunately Mr. Stevens was a bit preoccupied."

I felt myself flush. "I'm sorry. I had no right to listen in."

My mom sighed. "If your listening in on that conversation

237

is the worst thing that happens to me today, I'm in very good shape." She shook her head and rubbed her eyes, though it was still barely afternoon. "Anyway, I'll deal with Kent. Somehow. How was your morning?"

"I didn't even get into Alex's room," I admitted. "It's like she had a cordon of her friends who decided their mission in life was to keep me away."

"What about after that?" she queried. "You just got home."

"I stopped by the church."

"Really." My mom raised her eyebrows. "I didn't see you in the sanctuary."

"I went to the chapel. I needed someplace quiet," I explained. "That girl Mia I told you about? I saw her there. She decided to join."

"That's great. If she'd like, I'll give her a call when her paperwork comes through. Or even before. You'll ask her?"

I nodded. "I had lunch with her in West Hollywood. I really like her. I think we're going to go to the movies this week."

"Is she fresh out of rehab too?" My mother gave me a look to say that she was just joking. I would have laughed if I hadn't had the same thought at some point in the morning.

"No. Totally clean-living. She's pretty religious, actually."

I saw my mother relax visibly. Some kids might be annoyed that their parents took such interest in who their friends were, but I thought it was nice that she cared.

"Well, have fun together," my mother advised me. "Unless you'd like to stay home and babysit your brother for the next year."

I got the implication immediately. "He's—"

"Grounded," she said. "For six weeks, not a year. I do give him some credit for climbing out his window and jumping ten feet to the ground, then hopping the fence at the bottom of the hill."

"He was highly motivated," I pointed out.

She nodded. "Yes, he was. Anyway, Nat, you did the right thing in having him tell us. I'm proud of you for that."

I swallowed hard, knowing the thing I'd done that she would not be proud of. "Thank you."

In our subsequent silence, the house was so quiet I could hear the ice maker in the freezer run through its cycle of dump cubes, fill with water, and reset.

"Where is everyone?" I wondered aloud.

My mom sighed again. "Your dad's in his office, writing a treatment for the movie of his book that I just guaranteed is not going to be made, and about to get his world rocked when I tell him about the conversation you just overhead. Your brother is sulking in his room. You already know why his world is rocked. Your sister is sulking in her room, because the girl she thought was her new best friend was hitting on your brother, and she's about to get her world rocked when she finds out that she's not going to be on TV. And you?" She pointed at me. "You're a social outcast for calling your dad for help to keep your new friend sober. Worlds rocked on all fronts. Including my own, I might add." She rubbed her eyes and pressed at her temples like she had a headache. "Yesiree," she went on. "Shelton family's debut in their new home? *Big* success."

I had nothing to add. She was right.

She rubbed her eyes again. "I'd better get to work on next week's sermon. I'm sure Kent will be out there grading it. He's probably on the phone right now to the church board." She reached out and put a hand on my left shoulder. "Natalie, sweetie? I take back what I said before. Harriet the Spy might be a better career choice than minister of the Church of Beverly Hills. Now, excuse me. I have to go write the sermon of my life."

I watched as she headed for her and my dad's room. I knew that in fifteen minutes, she'd be in her favorite sweats, sprawled on the floor with yellow legal pads around her.

She hadn't gone more than ten feet, though, when her cell rang. She stopped and dug it out automatically, then smiled when she saw the caller ID. "It's from Mankato," she declared. "Donna Thiessen." My mother mustered more enthusiasm than I'd heard from her all day in her greeting to our old friend. "Donna! It's so great to hear from you!"

I started to move away, to let my mom have some privacy—especially after my earlier listening in—but she motioned for me to stay. I found myself again party to a conversation that was not my own, this time one where I had to fill in the ellipses in my mind.

"Yes, yes . . . everyone's well," my mother told Donna. "We're—we're okay. . . . Uh-huh. . . . Yes, you said something about that last time. . . . Uh-huh . . . Yes . . . I told you I wasn't . . . It's that bad with the new minister, is it?"

My mother edged against a doorframe as I paid close attention.

"Uh-huh . . . no hope, really? But maybe if you gave him

more time . . ." She was silent for quite a long time after that. As Donna talked, Mom nodded thoughtfully, completely engrossed.

So was I, because I got the gist of what Donna might be talking about. I remembered that the last time she'd called, she had wanted us to come home to Minnesota. This seemed like the same conversation, only more intense. The difference was that where my mom had been emotionally for the last call might not be where she was now. In fact, I knew it wasn't.

"Uh-huh . . . Uh-huh . . . I'm flattered that you'd try again, Donna. I'm not saying yes, and I'm not saying no, either. I think I owe it to the rest of my family to discuss this offer with them. Now, you're sure about this? . . . Got it. You're sure. . . . Well, you've given us all a great deal to think about. Goodbye, Donna. I'll call you as soon as I can."

She clicked off. "You got what that was about."

"I did." My mouth was dry. Very dry.

My mother nodded thoughtfully. "Well, I have a sermon to finish, and then this family has a decision it has to make. We came here as a family; we'll decide this as a family. Family meeting. Eight o'clock tonight. To decide whether to go home. Tell your brother and sister. Tell them to think about this like they've never thought about anything else in their lives."

That was it. My mom went into her bedroom, and I drifted into the kitchen, taking a Red Delicious apple from the fruit bowl and polishing it with the bottom of my shirt just for something to do.

I was stunned. There was an actual chance that we would be going back to Minnesota. How did I feel? At that moment, alone in the kitchen, with my sister sulking, my brother sulking, my mother overworked and browbeaten, and my father about to get his heart broken, with my new friend in the hospital and me a social outcast, how did I feel? I had a chance to go home. How do you think I felt?

Yes. That's how I felt. Once again, I knew exactly what I needed to do.

Chapter Twenty-Three

I *was* going to see Alex, and no guardians of the gates of hell in designer clothes, also known as Alex's friends, were going to stop me.

That didn't mean I couldn't use backup. So before I drove back to Cedars-Sinai, I stopped and talked one more time to Shep. He was so ticked that I hadn't been able to see his sister that he called the nurse's station and told them in no uncertain terms that whenever Natalie Shelton came to the hospital, she was to be escorted into Alex's room, and any other visitors were to be escorted out. He might be under house arrest, but he was still Alex's legal guardian. If he heard that his instructions were not being followed, they'd hear from his lawyer.

As it turned out, none of that was necessary. Either the Brooke squad was on a late-lunch-and-drinks-at-the-Ivy break, or they'd simply had enough. The hall outside Alex's room was empty, and her door was open.

I peered inside. No one was there beside Alex. She was sleeping, so I shuffled in as quietly as I could. I'd brought with me once again both the photograph of her parents and Twitch the rabbit. As I entered, I tried to figure out where to put them. I decided to lean the photograph on the nightstand so it faced her, and arranged the stuffed rabbit next to her head, on the pillow.

When they were in place, I looked at Alex. Really looked at her. Her hair was pulled back off her face in a ponytail. Without makeup, she appeared no older than fourteen. A battered fourteen. There was a bruise on her left cheekbone and another above her right eye, probably from the airbag that had to have deployed at the moment of impact. An IV drip ran into her right arm; there was an oxygen monitor clipped to her manicured right forefinger. Her color was better than I'd expected for someone who'd just had her spleen removed. I smiled ruefully at the thought of that. She wasn't going to be happy with the scar on her abs.

"Alex?"

I breathed her name as softly as I could, watching the consistent rise and fall of her chest under the thin blue hospital blanket and sheet.

No answer. She was really sleeping, not just resting in the twilight zone from the pain meds that had to be dripping through the IV.

I tried one more time, in case she was on the verge of coming back to the world. "Alex?"

Nothing.

Crap. This would have to be a monologue—a monologue

that probably wouldn't even register with her. I needed to do it anyway. I just wasn't sure if it was for her or for me. Maybe it was for both of us. There was an ugly blue plastic chair near the window. I quietly retrieved it and sat by her bedside.

"Alex? It's me. Natalie. This is the second time I've come to see you. I want you to know that there are lots of people who care about you, who've been here, too. I saw your brother twice today. He's not allowed to come to the hospital, or else he'd be here all the time. He loves you so much.

"Chloe is fine at camp. Shep thinks you should call her in a day or two, tell her that you were in an accident but that you're going to be fine and she should just enjoy the summer. So don't worry about her."

I took a deep breath and exhaled slowly. What else?

"I am so, so sorry about last night. I blew it. I said I'd help you stay sober and I didn't. I'm well aware that if you were awake, you would say I was being ridiculous, that what you did was of your own free will, and that I ought to just shut up. I know you. I still got caught up in my own drama and let you down. I'm sorry for that, and I'll always be sorry. I hope that you can find a way to forgive me."

I stopped again. Should I tell her that I had a big family meeting that night? That we might treat this time in Beverly Hills the way I was treating my escapade on the floor of the cabin with Sean? That is, like it never happened?

"My family is thinking about going home," I continued softly. I reached for the stuffed rabbit, Twitch, without realizing it and held it to my chest as if it was my own cherished childhood object. "I don't know what we'll decide. But I can tell you that right now I think I've had enough. I'll let you know. I promise. Get well, Alex. Just get well. I miss you."

There were tears on my cheeks as I kissed her gently on the forehead and placed Twitch an inch from her left temple. Then I closed my eyes and said a quick, heartfelt prayer for God to give wisdom and strength to her doctors and for her to get well—in every sense of that word—as fast as she could.

That was it. I kissed her again and took my leave, glancing back one more time when I reached the door. She slept peacefully. No sign of the demons that I knew tormented her.

Now what? There was still three and a half hours until the big family meeting. Not sure where I was heading, I left Alex's room, turned toward the elevator, and nearly smacked into someone coming toward me.

Brett Goldstein. Dressed in jeans and a plaid button-down, with his left arm in a sling. Other than being kind of pale, he looked fine.

"Hi" was his greeting.

"Hi" was mine.

He had the same effect on me as always. Various internal organs, including my heart, rearranged themselves. I told my heart to play dead. Brett was just like the rest of Brooke's friends. Jaded. Self-absorbed. Very, very selfish.

"How is she?" He shoved one hand in his jeans pocket.

"Asleep. I didn't talk to her at all." I could hear the edge in my voice and I liked it, knowing that Brett had to hear it, too.

He nodded thoughtfully but said nothing more.

I folded my arms. "How about you?"

"They're going to release me. My elbow is sprained, hence the sling. They thought for a while I had a concussion, but when I counted backward from a thousand by sevens, they decided my brain was fine."

I frowned. "Brain, maybe. Judgment? The jury's out."

He frowned back at me. "You're pissed about last night."

I stared at him. "You should have known better than to take Alex to Hollywood!"

It came out angrier and more emotional than I had intended, but I didn't care.

His eyes blazed as he fired back. "Hey, I wasn't drinking, and I wasn't going to drink. I was there to keep an eye on her—which you could have found out if you'd merely asked!"

"You drove, didn't you? *Didn't* you?" I said accusingly. "You took her where you knew—"

"I'm her friend, not her father. Alex makes her own choices."

Our voices carried down the hall to the nursing station, and I saw Nurse Ratched, who was still on duty, stick her disapproving head out of a patient's room and glare at us.

I shook my head. "We can't talk here. We could wake her."

"Follow me."

He motioned down the hall, and I trailed him past the nurses' station. Just past the double bank of elevators was a small lounge with two couches, a stuffed chair, a water dispenser, a utilitarian wall clock that read 4:31 p.m., and a wall-mounted television tuned silently to a Dodgers game. He sank into a navy blue faux leather couch. I sat next to him.

247

"Here's what I don't get," I said, only slightly mollified. "Last night we had a plan. Why didn't you answer your cell? I tried you like a dozen times."

"Forgot to charge it. It was out of juice by the time we split up to look for her. Only I didn't know it," he replied.

I felt like strangling him. "That's your excuse? You could have *borrowed* someone's phone."

"Yeah," he agreed. "But that would assume I know your number by heart. Which I don't."

If he was telling the truth about his battery running out, he had a point. But . . .

"How about using Alex's phone from the car?" I asked, challenging him.

He looked at me cockeyed. "Are you kidding? You called her. She didn't want to pick up, and let you go to voice mail. You have to know that. She wouldn't let me touch her phone."

If that was true, he had another point, but I wasn't ready to give up.

"You understand why I'm so upset with you?"

He rubbed his cheek. "Look, Nat, you're making a lot of judgments here about people you don't really know. You don't know much about Alex, you don't know much about me, and you definitely don't know much about life in Los Angeles. I wish I had your number memorized. It would have made a difference. But the fact is, Alex is old enough to make her own decisions, whether you like those decisions or not."

I folded my arms again, feeling the tension in my muscles.

"Yes," I said. "To a point. Here's the point: when you care about someone and they're doing something self-destructive, you have a *responsibility* to help them."

"That's how *you* see it." Brett winced and readjusted the sling. "Here's how *I* see it. Alex drinks, she doesn't drink. She parties, she doesn't party. That's her call. Whether I decide to drive her or not, that's my call. Not your call. And *definitely* not your father's call."

I flushed. "Someone told you." Not that I was surprised.

"Someone told a lot of people. Phoning him? Bad move. Astonishingly bad move, actually."

I felt my jaw tighten. "I'd risk having all of Alex's so-called friends hate my guts before I'd risk her life. That's what *real* friends do."

"Maybe that's the way it's done back in Minnesota," Brett said. "But it's not the way we do it here."

"That doesn't make your way the right way. Maybe you guys could stand to learn a thing or two about values."

He glowered for a moment like he was going to let me have it, but then shrugged. "Maybe. And maybe you guys could stand to learn a thing or two about self-righteousness. Anyone ever tell you you've got quite the streak going on?"

Oh, he was making me insane. Somehow, he had turned this into a discussion of my character flaws?

"You're an idiot." I jumped up, prepared to walk out on him.

He stood, too, and used his good arm to hold me fast. My face was inches from his. His eyes pinned me. "I think you're a terrific girl, Nat. Smart, thoughtful, loyal, caring. And pretty. No, not pretty. Beautiful."

He thought I was beautiful? With his good hand still holding my arm, his eyes softened.

"I'm not perfect, Natalie. Never claimed to be. Don't even *want* to be."

I softened, too. "I guess I feel like . . . like what we're supposed to do is try to be our best selves."

He pursed his lips enigmatically. "Fine. I accept you the way you are. I can deal with it."

Actually, he didn't know me at all. I had a mental flash to me and Sean entwined on the world's ugliest rug, and the aftermath. My acting like it had never happened, and then my judging Sean for not being willing to open himself to me emotionally.

"I've made a few mistakes," I admitted.

"Who hasn't?" Brett finally let go of my arm. "I've got to get back downstairs. My parents are waiting to sign me out. Want to ride down with me?"

I did. But I wanted to go back and look in on Alex again. Brett nodded when I told him that. He understood. "You still have my number?"

"Yeah," I said.

We stood together in silence. For a brief moment, I thought he was going to kiss me. And in that moment, I wanted him to. Even if it was a kiss goodbye, I wanted the experience of being kissed by Brett Goldstein. It might be the only chance I would ever get.

That wasn't what happened. Instead of moving his lips to mine, he took a step or two backward and told me to call him. "If you don't, Natalie? Put it on your list of mistakes."

With that, he turned and loped to the elevators. I didn't move until I saw him get into an open one.

When I got back to Alex's room, she was still asleep; the Brooke squad was still nowhere around. I went inside, scrawled a quick note to her on a napkin I found, and tucked it under Twitch. It wasn't easy to leave that note, to say what I had to say, but I did it.

Chapter Twenty-Four

Eight p.m. Family meeting.

I had thought that we would do it at the kitchen table at Ricardo's mansion, since whenever we'd had big family discussions in Mankato, the venue was always the wooden kitchen table my father had inherited when his parents had last moved. There was a ritual to the thing, no matter how heavy or serious. We would assemble. My father would sit in the chair closest to the refrigerator, with my mom to his left and then us three kids completing the circle, in birth order. Before the meeting, my mother would have put bowls of shelled hazelnuts and pretzels in the center of the table for easy nibbling, plus pitchers of apple juice and ice water.

Whoever had called the meeting would speak first. Then the rest of us would chime in. Sometimes we'd just share our feelings. Other times, we'd actually take a vote.

The funny thing is, as I think back on those meetings

where we did vote, I remember that the tally was always unanimous . . . right up until the four-to-one vote to move to California.

This meeting was different. Different setting, and different outcome. Neither kitchen table, nor unanimous, nor four-to-one.

Start with the setting. My parents drove us to a neutral location. Will Rogers State Beach, at the western end of Sunset Boulevard, where Temescal Canyon Road dead-ends into the Pacific Coast Highway in the town of Pacific Palisades. If you turn north on the highway, you'll be in Malibu; south takes you to Santa Monica.

Even though we arrived at 7:45 p.m., hundreds of people were still on the sand, doing all kinds of beachy things. There was Frisbee throwing, there were several games of beach volleyball under way, including one of Olympic quality, and at least a dozen surfers were in the water, waiting for the perfect wave to ride. The sun was low in the sky, framed by puffy cumulus clouds that promised a spectacular sunset. Terns wheeled over the waves, and a slight onshore breeze tousled our hair.

I carried the beach blanket. Chad had the drinks. Gemma brought the nuts and pretzels. My parents followed us. From the time they'd told us that we were going to the beach to the time we'd arrived, they'd had nothing to say. En route, neither of my siblings had much to say, either. For that matter, neither did I.

We found a clear spot of sand and spread out the blanket. A hundred feet to our left, a young couple on a gray quilt macked without coming up for air. Close to the waterline were three girl surfers resting up for one last assault on the water. They looked sleek and confident in their wet suits. I felt anything but sleek and confident.

We passed around the drinks and the nuts, and my mom, as always, started us with a prayer. Then she was silent. Nothing sounded but the waves and the terns. In that quiet, though, I understood why my parents had brought us here instead of convening us in a mansion that was not our own. This beach, this sunset—they belonged to everyone.

We waited. Mom had called the meeting; she'd start.

"Okay. Let's begin." Mom looked around the circle, taking in each of our faces. "You know the issue. We've been here in Los Angeles for less than two weeks. Part of it has been good, and part of it hasn't been so good."

"You can say that again," Gemma muttered, shooting Chad a hateful look.

"You'll get your chance, Gem," my father warned.

"It's fine, Charlie," Mom assured him. "Meanwhile, back home, our church hasn't had an easy time of it with the pastor who replaced me. Bottom line—you know this already—they've made an offer for us to come home. We wouldn't have to be back until the start of the school year, which would give us time to travel. Basically, we can do what we want for two months."

"I could go right back to school at Mankato East?" Gemma asked.

"Yes," my father told her. "No problem."

My mother cleared her throat. "Come September, it would

254

be like we'd never been away. Donna Thiessen has already been in touch with our tenants. If we pay for the movers, they're willing to move. The church said they'll handle that expense."

I hadn't heard that part, which meant that my mother had to have had another conversation with Donna while I was out for the afternoon. That conversation had gotten very specific, evidently.

"Charlie?" My mom put her left hand on my dad's arm. "What do you think?"

My father frowned. "Mixed feelings. There's a lot about this place that's good—even great—for you, Marsha, people like Kent Stevens notwithstanding."

"But what about you, Dad?" Gemma asked.

My dad nodded. "I'm disappointed about my book. But there are other producers here who could turn it into a movie. Or not."

"That's an argument to stay," my mom said.

My dad frowned more deeply. "Kind of. But the fact is, I'm worried about the kids, Marsha. Really worried. After last night, especially."

"You don't have to worry about me," Chad insisted.

"Which is exactly why I'm worried," my dad went on. "And right now, I have the floor. Well, the blanket."

His eyes swung to all three of us. "I've been watching you guys, and I don't like what I'm seeing. I figure it'll only get worse." He turned back to Mom. "If it were just us two, I'd stay if that was what you wanted. But it isn't just us. I vote we go home."

"I vote we stay." Chad came in so fast that it was almost like there was no period on the end of my dad's last sentence.

"You would," Gemma sneered.

"It's not about Lisa," Chad declared.

"Ha!" Gemma barked. "But what am I laughing for? She's laughing at me! She only pretended to like me to get—"

"It was a clip for YouTube!" Chad fired back.

"Sure, but what are you guys going to do for an encore? A clip for Vivid Video?" Gemma folded her arms and scowled at him, then swung toward my mother. "Just in case you're wondering, I vote we go home. Yesterday. I hate it here. Everyone sucks."

Wow. To think that of our entire family, she'd been the one who had most wanted to move to Los Angeles. It showed how deeply she'd been hurt. I wondered if there was more than she was admitting, more than feeling betrayed by her new best friend and losing a walk-on part on a television show. In Mankato, Gemma was a rare beauty who stood out in any crowd. Here? There were beautiful girls on every corner. She wasn't special at all, and she wouldn't be until she learned to be special in ways that had nothing to do with appearance.

So. It was two to one in favor of outta here. I glanced westward. The setting sun painted the clouds pink and purple. The chick surfers were paddling out in the last light of day. So easy, so carefree. Life in Mankato used to be like that. I missed it. So much.

"Nat?" My mom's voice got my attention.

"Yeah?"

"Are you ready?"

"I'll take my pass," I replied.

You were allowed to do that—pass one time—at family meetings if you weren't quite ready to speak. I wanted to hear what else Mom had to say before I talked. Possibly, if she voted in favor of leaving, she would make what I had to say moot. There'd be three votes to go, and that would be that.

"Okay, then." My mom looked directly at me as she talked. "I didn't raise you kids to be quitters. I am certainly not a quitter. Yes, there are a lot of challenges that come with this territory. Yes, there's a lot that we're not used to. Yes, people are different out here. Very different." She turned to Chad, who got busy studying the blanket. "I'm not saying there won't be bumps along the way. But I have full confidence you kids can be your true selves anywhere. With God's help, your father and I can do the same."

She and my father shared a tender glance. "If it's up to me? We stay." She fixed her eyes on me. "Which means, Nat, it's up to you."

I gulped. That was not what I had been hoping for. Early in the day, I'd been sure of what I wanted. Now I was sure of nothing but my love for my family.

Gemma pleaded with eyes that said *Let's go home*.

Chad's eyes implored me: *Let's stay*.

My father, who would make the best of it either way, ready to leave.

My mother, open to whatever I had to say, but obviously hoping I'd agree with her.

What did I want? There were so many reasons to go home, and so few reasons not to.

Then, on the wind, in a wave, in the caw-caw of a tern, I heard Mia's voice from that afternoon in the chapel. How had she gotten through it? I'd asked her. Her mom's death, the utter upheaval in her life?

"I suppose faith never makes sense, really. It's something your heart tells you is true. You can't prove it, but you believe anyway. And sometimes, Natalie? Sometimes faith is all we've got."

My mom had that kind of faith. Did I?

"I think . . ." I took a deep breath. "I think there's a reason we're here, even if we're not sure what it is. I vote we stay."

"What?" Gemma exploded.

"Yes!" Chad pumped a happy fist in the air.

I dead-eyed him. "I'm not doing this for you."

"You're sure, Natalie?" My dad checked in with me.

No. I wasn't sure. But I'd made my decision and I wasn't changing my mind.

My mom stretched and then smiled gently. "Well, then. I guess we're staying. I don't know about you guys, but I want to take a walk down to the water. How about we meet back at the car in fifteen minutes? Gemma and Chad, you guys can pack up? Charlie, you coming?"

Gemma's eyes were slits of anger, but she nodded as my parents stood and started hand in hand across the sand to the waterline.

"I won't forget this," Gemma told me.

"Me neither," Chad quipped, with an entirely different tone.

I really didn't want to get into any more with either one of them. "I'll see you guys at the car."

"Where are you going?" Gemma demanded.

"Walking. Alone."

I picked up my small backpack and started south through the sand, past the make-out couple still at full throttle. When I'd voted, I'd had a sense of what I was getting myself into. But now, as I made my way toward the breaking waves, the enormity of my decision washed over me like the surf itself. I hadn't had a real conversation with Alex since the accident. When would she get well? Would she even get well? What would it be like when we talked? The note I had left her read *God is watching us*. What would she think of that? How would she treat me? She could hate me. Her friends did. They had to have a lot of power at my new school. I was in for a miserable time. No doubt about it.

There were Gemma and Chad. Each of them had ample reason to hate me. Maybe things would improve with them over time. Maybe they wouldn't. Much depended on what happened with Lisa Stevens—how she would treat them. And much of what happened with Lisa Stevens depended on what happened with Kent Stevens, who was furious with my mother. My mother is a pretty tough cookie. You don't work as a minister without getting one or more of your parishioners angry at you. But Kent Stevens was no ordinary parishioner. He had a lot of power. How would he use it? If our church back in Minnesota was ready to fire its new minister and rehire my mother, would Kent possibly want to take the same route with my mom? That thought was frightening. Maybe our staying here in Los Angeles wasn't even up to us.

There was Sean, and there was Brett. If I was going to be

the person I wanted to be, I would have to own the truth with each of them, face to face, whatever that truth turned out to be.

Those were all daunting thoughts. Just as I'd thought of Mia's words about faith when I'd made my decision about how to vote, I thought of Mia now. I had to have faith that more would be revealed to me about all those things. That more would be revealed to all of us.

I stopped at the water's edge. A few hundred yards up the beach, I could see my mom and dad silhouetted against the setting sun. Their arms were around each other. I marveled at that. They'd disagreed about this decision. Yet they were still together, still in love. I hoped that one day, with God's help, I could have that, too. Maybe I'd even write a song about it.

I took out my cell. There were three texts I knew I needed to send. The first was to Sean.

S—CALL ME IN THE A.M. ABOUT YR TRIP. IMPT. N

The second was to Mia.

MIA—MOVIE WED NITE GOOD FOR ME. NAT

The last one? To Brett.

BRETT: STILL READY FOR DINNER. NAME THE
NIGHT. NAT

Sent.

As I looked out at the last rays of the day, the clouds

dappled by patches of colors so fluid and beautiful they quickened my heart, I didn't know if I'd done the right thing in opting to stay. I knew this much, though: I wanted to live honestly. Authentically.

My cell beeped. I looked at it. A text. From Brett.

NAT: FRI EVA RESTAURANT, 8 PM. CAN'T WAIT.
BRETT.

I was excited, and at the same time scared to death.
Sounds a lot like life.